A Case Of
Timber Treachery

BRUCE BRADBURN
Illustrations by Rhys Haug

BOOK PUBLISHERS NETWORK

Book Publishers Network
P.O. Box 2256
Bothell • WA • 98041
PH • 425-483-3040
www.bookpublishersnetwork.com

Copyright © 2014 by Bruce Bradburn

All rights reserved. No part of this book may be reproduced, stored in, or introduced into a retrieval system, or transmitted in any form, or by any means (electronic, mechanical, photocopying, recording, or otherwise) without the prior written permission of the publisher.

10 9 8 7 6 5 4 3 2 1

Printed in the United States of America

LCCN 2014947381
ISBN 978-1-940598-43-7

Editor: Julie Scandora
Cover design: Laura Zugzda
Interior design: Melissa Vail Coffman
Production: Scott Book

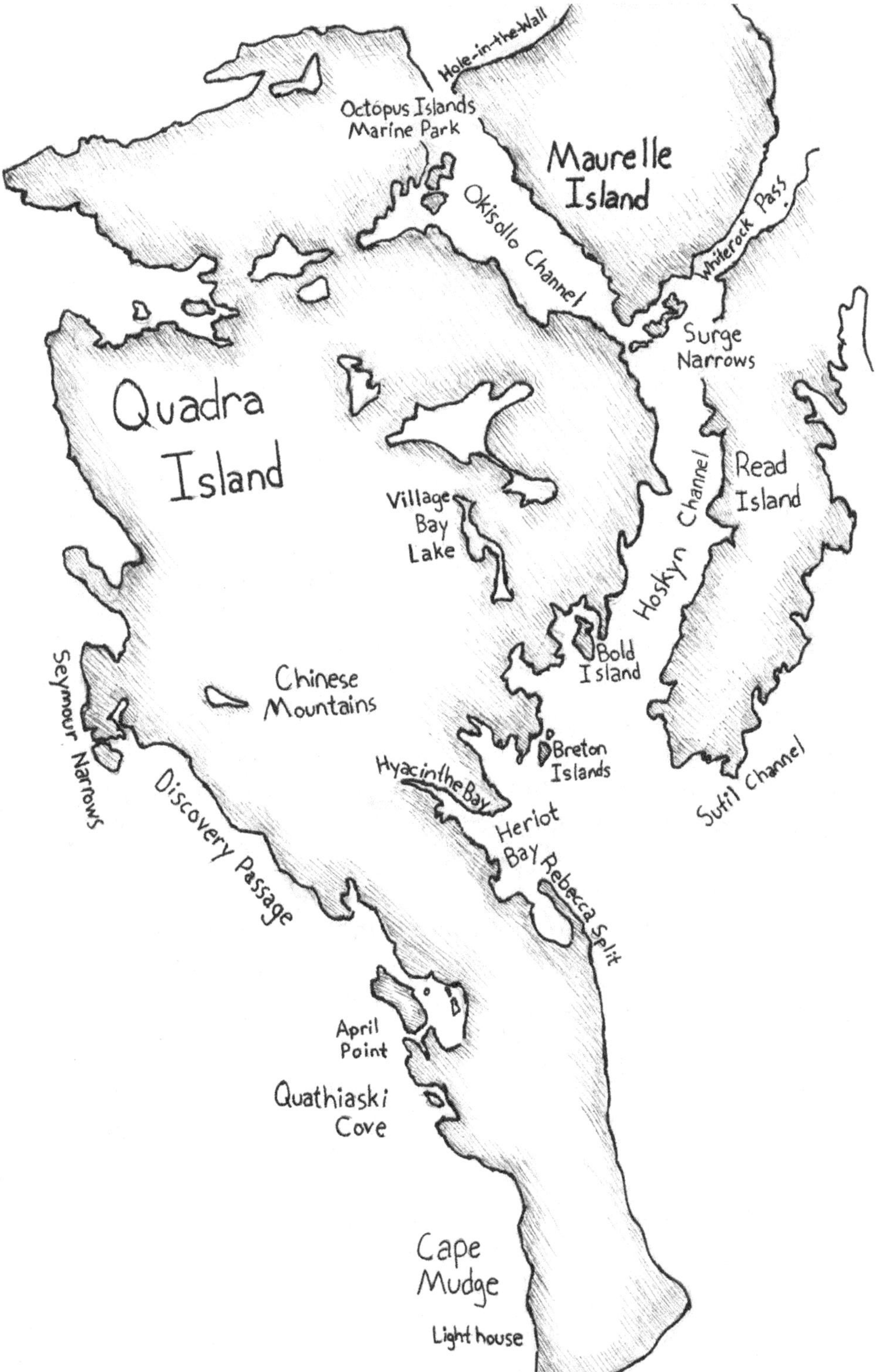
Hole-in-the-Wall
Octopus Islands
Marine Park
Maurelle
Island
Okisollo Channel
Whiterock Pass
Surge
Narrows
Quadra
Island
Read
Island
Hoskyn Channel
Village
Bay
Lake
Bold
Island
Seymour Narrows
Chinese
Mountains
Breton
Islands
Hyacinthe Bay
Heriot
Bay
Rebecca Split
Sutil Channel
Discovery Passage
April
Point
Quathiaski
Cove
Cape
Mudge
Light house

Acknowledgements

The author wishes to acknowledge the valuable information on logging in British Columbia provided by Mark Nighswander, a Quadra Island resident and logger who also operates the Quadra Island Deer Farm.

Mark's insights into the local timber industry, its rules and regulations, as well as its practices, was vital in putting together a coherent picture for this story. Several of his humorous tales regarding log theft have been incorporated, although with a certain amount of literary license.

The author also wishes to acknowledge the support and encouragement from his wife, Meg, and the rest of his family.

There is no way this story could have seen the light of day without the efforts of the entire team at Book Publishers Network, and those efforts are greatly appreciated.

Chapter One

Will had spent much of his fall getting re-acclimated to the big-city life of downtown Chicago. He and his parents had had an amazing visit with his cousin, Michael, and his parents at their home on Quadra Island in British Columbia last summer. The two cousins had experienced an adventure with potentially disastrous results but had survived due to the quick thinking of a number of people, including their parents.

Upon his return, Will had settled into a new school year with his old friends and usual activities, but things had certainly changed for him.

Some things had not changed, however; the Cubs did not win the pennant, in spite of being in first place when he returned home. As fall wore on into winter, the snows came, the lake froze, and the Bears wound up behind the Packers. They even lost a key game to the Seahawks, which kept them out of the playoffs. As the basketball and hockey seasons ramped up, the Bulls gave no signs of returning to the glory years of Michael Jordan, and the Blackhawks appeared destined for the middle of their division.

For Will, though, professional sports had lost some of its fascination. He still played on the JV teams for the Chicago Latin School and enjoyed the competition and being with his buddies, but his new-found friendship with his cousin, Michael, was now a special part of his life.

The two corresponded via email on almost a daily basis on every subject imaginable, but they always ended up discussing what they would do on Quadra Island the next time they got together. They were quite careful in their communications not to make direct reference to the details of their part in breaking up a burglary ring on the island since the people involved had serious ties to organized crime, and the local authorities had warned them about being conspicuous.

The warnings were not really necessary since both Will and Michael fully realized that they had been within minutes of being dumped at sea in the middle of the night by some extremely bad guys who had no reservations about "taking care of" a couple of nosy teenagers.

What the boys did discuss was how next summer they would see if their parents would let them take the Whaler out on their own, maybe even for some overnight camping trips on the nearby islands. They pored over maps and navigation charts they brought up online and put together plans for explorations.

One night in mid-February, just as spring training was getting started (this being "Next Year" for the Cubs), Will was at dinner with his parents, Doug and Judy, in their condo on Lake Shore Drive, when the subject of another trip west in the summer came up. This time, Mom and Dad had no trouble convincing Will to make the trip.

"I suppose you might like to make another trip to Seattle and Quadra this coming summer?" his father asked Will.

"You bet!"

"Well, your mom and I are putting our schedules together to work it in right around the time you get out of school. This year I won't be able to take a whole month, but Bob and Angie have already told us that you are more than welcome to stay the entire summer."

"That's totally awesome! Michael and I have already been talking about some adventures we want to have."

"Let's try to leave the Mafia out of them this year," put in his mother.

"No problem; once was enough," agreed Will.

Chapter One

"You finish school the first week of June, so let's shoot for the week after that," his dad suggested.

"Gosh, that's almost four months away," said Will. "You don't suppose we could make a trip out during spring break?"

"I'm afraid that's not in the cards. I do have to work for a living, you know. I assume you still want a roof over your head and meals on the table, unless you just bought the winning ticket in the lottery."

"I'm not eighteen; they won't let me buy tickets—but you could."

"Let's return to reality here," said Judy. "Four months will go by so fast you won't even realize it."

"I guess it will at that," said Will. "I'm really having to hit the books hard this year, and I do have JV basketball and baseball coming up, so I'm not going to be just sitting around thinking about summer. Besides, Michael and I will be laying out some plans for trips on our own."

"In that regard," said his father, "I will contact Bob about what may be required for you two to use the boat, assuming that's OK with him and Angie. I'm pretty sure some sort of license is required, and you don't have any experience with powerboats, although you certainly mastered the kayaks last summer. As you noticed on a couple of the boat trips we took last year, those waters can be extremely dangerous if you don't know what you're doing."

"I don't think we will venture too far away, and I do know what you are talking about, so we will be careful."

After dinner, Will went to his room to do his homework, but did have time to fire off one short email to Michael.

Chapter Two

Out in Seattle, Michael was sitting at his desk just before dinner working on a lengthy algebra assignment when Will's email popped up in his inbox. The math was going pretty well, so he decided he could take some time off to read it.

Hi cuz,

I'm totally hyped about the trip out this summer. Really think your folks would let us use the Whaler on our own?

Will

Michael typed back:

Hey Will,

I'll ask tonight. Never know till we ask. I'm sure they'll be cool with it—long as we don't go too far away. We'd have our cells and the radio, in case we don't have coverage.

Michael

Chapter Two

He had just hit Send when the aroma of fresh baked bread came wafting into his room. He took one slight look at his algebra paper, decided he could finish up in less than an hour, pushed back his chair, and headed for the kitchen.

The oven door was still open when he walked in, and he could see that his mother, Angie, had two beautiful loaves of bread out cooling on the counter.

"Ah, I see your sense of smell is fully intact," she said with a smile. "The mac and cheese is going into the oven right now, and it should be done by the time the bread cools down enough to slice. The salad is all made, and I thought we could just have some ice cream with frozen raspberries for dessert. Does that suit you?"

"Mom, you never disappoint," Michael said enthusiastically. "Can I help by setting the table? I'm taking a little break from algebra, but I'll finish it as soon as we're through dinner."

"That would be lovely. Your father just pulled into the driveway, so we should be ready to eat in about half an hour. We can just eat here at the kitchen table tonight."

Michael got out the silverware and napkins and placed them on the table, along with the salad tongs, glasses, and plates. He was getting the salad dressing and milk container from the refrigerator when his father came in from the garage.

"Hi there, you two," he said, giving Angie a kiss on the cheek and taking a playful poke at Michael's shoulder. "It sure smells good in here. I hope we're getting close to dinner; I'm famished!"

"Less than half an hour," said Angie.

"Perfect. How was school today, Michael?"

"Same ol' same ol'. I have a big math assignment, but I'm almost finished. If I get it done right after dinner, do you think we might be able to work in one quick game of Monopoly before lights out?"

"I make all games 'quick.' Are you sure you're ready for the bitter taste of defeat?" said Bob.

"I think I can somehow bear up under the pressure, Dad."

"If you two are through posturing, why don't you wash your hands and come to the table?"

A few minutes later, all three were seated with a steaming casserole of mac and cheese, a fresh green salad, and a still-warm loaf of bread before them. When he had finished his first helping and was ready to start on his second, Michael asked, "Do you think it would be possible for Will and me to take the boat out on our own this summer—maybe even on an overnighter?"

"It's funny you should mention it. Just before I left work, I got a call from Doug asking the same question. I can't imagine you and Will have been discussing this, right?"

"Of course we have. What do you think?"

"Well, I know you've had a little experience with the Whaler when I've been with you, but that's quite a bit different from being out on your own in those waters."

"We would be careful."

"It's not just that. You would both need a license. They're called Pleasure Craft Operator Cards, or PCOCs, and are required to operate a motorized vessel in BC. If you get caught without a card, it's a $250 fine."

"Wow, that's harsh."

"Not really, they're just trying to keep boating safe for everyone. It costs about forty dollars to get your license. You can take the exam online, and the card is good forever. There's an online study guide you can check out, as well as some sample questions. The exam itself is fifty questions long, and they're multiple choice. When you pass, you can print out a temporary card; they mail your permanent one in a couple of weeks. If you don't pass the test, you can retake it without paying another fee."

"Gee, Dad, you sure know a lot about it."

"I had to get my card before I could run the boat. I didn't want a $250 fine, either. Regardless of your plans for this summer, you and Will may as well take a shot at the exam anyway. At some point, you'll be piloting the boat and will need the card. I'll even give you some incentive to study for the exam. If you pass it on the first try, I'll pay the fee. If it takes more times, you will have to pay. I'll talk to Doug to see if he'll match the offer for Will."

"Cool, thanks! Does that mean we can go off by ourselves?"

"Don't rush it. Pass the test, get your cards—both of you—and we can discuss it in more detail. I am sure your mothers will want to have some input."

"OK, that's fair. Point me to the website, and I'll get right on it!"

"Why don't you finish your dinner and your math first? There's no hurry about the card; we're months away from heading up. Besides, I need to give you and your mom a Monopoly lesson."

Michael did finish his dinner AND his algebra, but before he joined his parents for the Monopoly "lesson," he had to shoot off an email to Will.

Hey Will,

I think they'll let us use the boat this summer. Our dads talked about it. We need to get our operator's license, but I think they'll be on board if we pass the test.

Michael

With this sent, Michael was off to the living room where the Monopoly board was already set up. Bob, as promised, delivered his patented lesson.

Chapter Three

Encouraged by the pledge from their fathers to cover the forty-dollar cost of the boating license exam, both Will and Michael devoted as much time as they could to studying the online material from BoatSafeCanada. However, with Michael involved in winter swimming and Will on the JV basketball team plus the increased academic load of ninth grade, the boys were really able to carve out some time only on the weekends.

They emailed each other to compare notes on the study guide knowing that each would have to take the online exam individually, but they were able to come up with a scheme to help each other out. They would study the same section and then prepare a test for each other on that section and email a set of questions. Going back to the study guide, they were able to grade each other's response.

After a month or so of this mutual testing, both boys felt they had mastered the basics of water safety and were prepared to take the real exam. They decided to do it at exactly the same time, accounting for the two-hour time difference, and were thrilled when they both achieved perfect scores.

Bob and Doug were more than happy to fulfill their part of the bargain and had a good feeling about their sons being able to operate the boat on their own. Even Angie and Judy were impressed and put at ease.

Chapter Three

Michael's father, however, wanted to see how well the written material had really prepared his son for handling a boat. Since the winter weather in Seattle was fairly mild, Bob was able to rent a Whaler for several weekend afternoons and take Michael out on Lake Washington for some sea trials.

These went extremely well, and in short order, Michael had mastered the handling and also the docking of the craft. Bob was pleased with his son's proficiency but reminded him numerous times that the calm waters of the lake were a far cry from what he might experience if caught in a storm or rough water up north. Michael had seen enough of the massive tidal currents and whirlpools to take his father's words to heart.

Will was not able to get the same kind of hands-on experience since the waters around Chicago in the winter remain frozen from December until sometimes as late as April.

However, Doug was able to procure manuals on the type of motor on the Whaler and had Will spend time studying the workings of an outboard motor. They were able to go to a local shop where the owner was happy to spend some time with Will, letting him get his hands dirty on some real engines.

By the time spring had rolled around, both families felt comfortable with the boys' abilities and had agreed that they would be allowed to go off on their own during the summer. They knew the cousins would train each other in what each had learned and both would become proficient with the boat on the water. Since the boat also had a radio, the parents knew the boys could always call for assistance should they run into something they could not handle themselves.

The summer trip was still a couple of months off, but both Will and Michael had little time to think much about it. Crew season had started for Michael, and Will was heavily into baseball. Final exams were looming large for both boys, but they did keep the prospect of summer adventures in the back of their minds.

Chapter Four

With just about six weeks left in the school year for Will, his social studies teacher announced to the class that they would be doing a short course of study on Native American tribes and customs. The teacher asked the class if anyone had even a little knowledge of the first inhabitants of the North American continent, other than something gleaned from Western movies.

Will, although not shy in class, was never one to volunteer much. However, at this question, he enthusiastically raised his hand.

"Well, Will, this is a bit of a surprise," his teacher said. "You do know I am not referring to the Cleveland Indians or the Washington Redskins?"

The class got a big laugh out of this reference to Will's well-known love of sports, but he coolly responded, "Last summer I spent almost three months with my cousin and his parents on Quadra Island in British Columbia. I did pick up some information about the First Nations peoples."

"First Nations?" his teacher asked.

"That's how they are referred to in Canada."

"Please give us a brief summary of what you learned."

"Well, there're many tribes in the area of the northwestern United States and southwestern Canada. I learned a little about the tribes in the area around Quadra Island and farther north. Many of their

Chapter Four

customs, dress, dances, and other ceremonies were documented on film around the turn of the last century by a man named Edward Curtis. In 1914, he made a motion picture called, at the time, *In the Land of the Headhunters*; the title was later changed to *In the Land of the War Canoes*. They show the movie at the cultural center on Quadra, and we went to see it."

"That is VERY interesting," said his teacher.

"What's even more interesting," said Will, excitedly, "is that the original film is right here in Chicago at the Art Institute. Maybe the whole class could see it as part of this study."

This announcement was greeted enthusiastically by the rest of the class, and the teacher said he would look into the possibility of a field trip to the Art Institute.

After class, a number of Will's friends gathered around him, fascinated by his story and wanting to know more. There were even a couple of cute girls from the class who had never given him the time of day before but were now rather interested. He decided to play this for all it was worth.

That night at dinner, he related his classroom experience, and his parents were duly impressed. He told them that Michael had informed him that there was an extensive collection of the Curtis photographs at the Rainier Club in Seattle and wanted to know if the family might be able to see them, assuming they were stopping over in Seattle on their way north in the summer.

"Let me check on that," said his dad. "I think the Rainier Club might be a reciprocal of the University Club here. If that's the case, we could even arrange to stay there if they have overnight rooms. It might be more fun that a regular hotel."

"Gosh, that would be great, Dad," said Will.

"I think that would be a very nice idea," put in Judy. "We've stayed at several other reciprocals over the years, and they're always very pleasant and unique."

"I'll check on it first thing tomorrow."

Chapter Five

Michael arrived home from his after-school crew practice to find their SUV parked in the driveway. This was rather unusual since his father usually did not get home from work until well after six. He put in long hours so he could take extended time in the summer to be at their place on Quadra. Michael entered the house with a certain uneasy feeling that things were not quite right. He found his parents sitting at the kitchen table with concerned looks on their faces.

"What's up? You're home early, Dad. Is something wrong?"

"Just a bit of a problem up north," his father answered. "I got a call from the contractor who built the caboose for us. He said the island was hit by a freak windstorm last night and there were trees down all over. He went by our place just to check it out and noticed that we had three rather large firs come down. Fortunately, not any of our buildings were damaged, but he said it'll take some serious clearing."

"Wow; I'm happy there wasn't damage to the house and caboose, but I bet it's a mess."

"We were just trying to figure out how to handle this when you came in," said his mother.

"The contractor gave me the name and number of someone who does logging on the island who could probably give us a hand with the cleanup. I haven't called him yet, but the contractor said this

Chapter Five

fellow might be willing to do the cleanup for the timber if the trees weren't too badly damaged or weren't rotten. I was just about ready to telephone the logger when you came in, so I guess I'd better get on this."

Bob went into the small office he kept at home to make the call while Michael and his mother stayed in the kitchen.

"This whole thing threw me off a bit this afternoon. I haven't even started to think about dinner."

"Mom, why don't we just order pizza tonight? There's that place just a couple of blocks away that makes really good ones, and I'll walk over and pick them up so you and Dad can figure out what to do."

"That's very considerate, Michael," said his mother. "I'm sure your father will appreciate it as well. I'll give the pizza place a call. What do you want on yours?"

"You know me, everything but the kitchen sink, and large."

"As usual, I'll get a separate one for your father and me, and you will probably eat part of that as well."

Angie placed the order and was told that the pizzas would be ready in about a half-hour, so Michael said he would go to his room and at least lay out his homework for the evening and then walk over to pick up their dinner.

With the two still-warm pizzas on the kitchen table, the three of them gathered around with plenty of napkins and had a somewhat subdued meal. Bob had had a long conversation with the logger referred by their contractor who agreed to go out and take a look at the property the next day. There was not much they could do until they heard back from the logger, so they just worried.

Chapter Six

When Bob came home from work the next night, he found Angie and Michael anxiously awaiting the news from the north.

"I did get the call from the logger, whose name is Mark, and he gave me a rundown on what's going to be needed. There will be significant cleanup of broken branches, both on the trees that came down and on the smaller trees and bushes that were smashed. He did say, however, that the basic trees are in good shape and that he could use them for lumber. He even said that the value of the lumber he could get out of the three large trees might more than offset the cleanup costs. If that were the case, we could even make some money on the deal."

"That's a relief," said Angie. "I could just imagine our getting a huge bill for the debris removal."

"I hope it doesn't foul up the feeling of the place," put in Michael.

"Mark said he would be extremely careful with the cleanup operation, and the trees that came down were fairly close to the road, so he didn't think he would have to drag the logs out, if we were willing to have him rent a crane to come over from Campbell River to lift the logs onto his truck."

"Well, all this sounds as if it isn't quite as bad as we imagined it would be," said Angie.

Chapter Six

"That's right," responded Bob. "However, I think I'll have to make a quick trip up to check on things and have a face-to-face conversation with Mark. I've already checked with Kenmore Air, and they're into their spring schedule and have daily flights to April Point, so I'll have to spend just one night. I was thinking of going up over this weekend."

"Dad, is there any chance I could go with you?" asked Michael.

"What's your homework situation? You're getting pretty close to finals."

"I have a couple of days before the weekend. I do know my assignments for Monday already. If I can get them all finished up, can I go?"

"I think that can be arranged. I'm sure we can always use an extra pair of hands."

"If you don't mind, I'll stay here," said Angie. "I don't really want to survey the scene of destruction. I just want to see it all cleaned up so I can figure out what new plantings I need to take care of when we get there."

"I'm off to my room and my homework," said Michael.

"I'll call Kenmore right now and make our reservations on the assumption that you'll get everything done. I'll see if we can go up Friday afternoon or early Saturday morning and then be back by Sunday late afternoon."

Chapter Seven

The field trip for Will's class to the Art Institute was a great success. The movie was enjoyed by all, and Will's teacher had made arrangements for an official of the institute to let them view some artifacts. The lady who showed them the masks, tools, baskets, and other items also gave a brief talk on the area and Edward Curtis.

The students, who were all used to handheld video cameras, were amazed at the description of the bulky equipment Curtis used and had to transport. She told them all his still shots were photographed on glass plates, which were quite heavy, as well as fragile. She also noted that he had to carry all his development chemicals and even made some of them from seaweed.

Will's teacher made the point to the class that each one of them had more photographic capability in their cell phones than Curtis possessed in his pack animals laden with equipment and that these massive changes in technology had come about in less than one hundred years. The students found this almost unbelievable; for them, the first lunar landing, thirty years before their births, was ancient history.

The lady from the Art Institute noted that Curtis had traveled extensively in the southwestern United States, as well, and taken many photographs there, too. Will mentioned to her that his cousin lived in Seattle and had told him of a large collection of Curtis photographs

Chapter Seven

at the Rainier Club in that city. She said she was well aware of that collection and it was probably the largest assemblage of original works by Curtis that existed.

The bus ride back to school was animated with everyone talking about what they had seen and been told. Will's teacher thanked him for the tip about the film and said it was one of the best field trips he had ever led.

At dinner that night, Will told his parents of the excursion to the Art Institute and what his teacher had said. Will's father told them he had checked and found out that the Rainier Club was a reciprocal of the University Club in Chicago and they would be staying there for a couple of days on their way north in the summer. Both Will and Judy were delighted with the news.

Will said he would email Michael and let him know and headed off to his room. He turned on his computer and was about to write his email when he thought about the technology lesson he had learned earlier in the day. *Gosh,* he thought, *not that long ago, if I wanted to send a message to my cousin halfway across the country, it would take weeks. Now it takes nanoseconds.*

With that mind-numbing thought, he began to type:

Hi cuz,

Guess what? Today my social studies class went to see the original movie we saw at the cultural center on Quadra last summer. Cool to see it again. We're staying at the Rainier Club on our way to your place this summer, so I'll get to see the whole collection of Curtis's photos. Can't wait to come out again. Looks as if we'll come a week or so after I get out of school. When are you all headed up?

Will

A click on Send, and the message was gone and sitting on his cousin's computer over two thousand miles away.

Chapter Eight

Will did not have to wait long for a reply. Michael was in the middle of his homework assignments but wanted to share his news with Will so took a few moments out to respond.

Hey Will,

That's neat you saw the movie again with your whole class. You must have come off as a bit of an expert.

I have some not so great news from here. A wind storm hit Quadra a couple of days ago and blew down three trees on our property. They didn't smash the house or our place, the caboose, but it's a big mess. Dad and I are flying up for an overnight this weekend to survey the damage and meet with a logger who is going to do the cleanup. I'll give you the scoop when I get back on Sunday.

Michael

Will's reply was almost instantaneous.

Chapter Eight

Hi cuz,

Ouch! That's awful. I want to hear what happened as soon as you get back. Glad the caboose escaped. It's such a great place to hang out.

Thanks for turning me on to the Curtis photos and movie. More than the expert. There's this VERY cute girl in my class who now thinks I'm pretty cool.

Will

Will left his room and went to tell his parents about Michael's news report and found them in the living room reading. They were quite disturbed by the story, and Doug said he would call his brother first thing in the morning to see if there was anything they could do but it sounded as if Bob had everything well in hand.

"I'm sure this is the last thing Bob wants as a reason to visit their place on the island," said Doug. "It's so beautiful. I hope that lovely setting isn't too badly damaged."

"I'll second that thought," said Judy, and Will readily agreed.

Will spent the rest of the week and weekend awaiting word from Michael on the storm damage, but at least he had a few things to keep his mind occupied. The cute girl from his class asked if he would help her with her assignment in social studies, and he was more than happy to oblige. As they spent study periods together, Will found her to be a pleasant person to be around, and he discovered he actually enjoyed having someone to share ideas about their homework.

The weekend provided one of those lovely spring days in Chicago with mild temperatures and almost no humidity. He got together with his friends in the park for several games of 500 but could not wait until Sunday evening to hear from his cousin.

Chapter Nine

Michael and his dad boarded the 9 A.M. Kenmore Air flight to April Point on Saturday morning. They were already booked on the 1:30 P.M. return flight the next day, so this would be a whirlwind visit. They slid up to the dock at the April Point Resort just a few minutes after the scheduled 11:30 arrival time.

As they walked up the ramp to the lodge, Bob said, "We didn't get a chance for much breakfast this morning. What say we stop here for a bite of lunch? I'll call the Quadra Taxi and have them pick us up in an hour."

"That's fine with me," replied his son, "But I'm pretty worried about the damage."

"Likewise, but let's eat now, in case we don't feel like it later."

They proceeded into the dining room and ordered. Bob called Mark, the logger they were to meet at their home, and told him they would be there in about an hour, and the meeting was set. The taxi was right on time, and fifteen minutes later, they pulled into their driveway. Mark's truck was already parked in front of the house.

After introductions, Mark suggested they do a walk-around to get an idea of what was going to be involved in the cleanup and removal. It was not as bad as they had thought it might be from first observation. Mark explained how he would do the branch removal by chipping up all the smaller ones and the damaged shrubs. The

Chapter Nine

wood chips would be spread around as ground cover, simplifying replanting. The larger branches would be cut up and hauled away, including those he would take off the three trunks he would remove for cutting into lumber.

Mark noted that two of the trees had actually been blown over leaving their roots attached. These could be cut to the maximum sizes for use as lumber. The one tree that had broken off still left enough to be useful, although it was not as valuable as the other two. He repeated his suggestion that they authorize him to bring over a crane from Campbell River to minimize further damage to the site when the logs were removed and loaded onto his truck for transport to the mill.

Bob readily agreed to the crane, not wanting to inflict additional damage to their beautiful surroundings, and asked for an estimate of the costs involved in the cleanup and removal and what offset there might be for the timber. Mark told him it appeared to him to be a straight-up deal but assured them that any amount above the cleanup costs he received for the timber, he would split with them. They shook hands on it, and Bob asked Mark to come into the house for a cup of coffee.

While the coffee was brewing, Michael had a chance to talk with Mark and get an idea about what it took to be a logger. Mark explained that for a small operation, such as he had, it was pretty hard to make a real living off it, so he needed to do other things.

"Back in the old days—fifty to sixty years ago—a one- or two-man hand-logging operation could provide a comfortable income. You could go to the government and get a license for literally miles of coastline on these islands up here. You couldn't use heavy equipment—just axes, saws, cables, and hand winches."

"That sounds like really hard work," said Michael.

"It was for a few hardy souls. But it's young man's work. You had to be in great shape. The last hand-logging license in the province was granted in 1965. Now all logging involves power equipment."

"I can see doing this on a big island like Quadra where you have roads and trucks, but how did they get the logs to the mill from more remote locations?"

"The trees were felled on the steep slopes of the islands and then slid down into the water. There, they were rafted together, and when there were enough to make it worthwhile, a tug was called in to tow the raft to a mill. The logs were all branded so the mill would know whose logs were whose."

"You mean branded, like cattle?"

"Yup, and we still do that, but the branding has changed a bit. In the old days, the brands were as simple as a number and an *X*, *Y*, or *Z*. Nowadays, they are more complex and include the woodlot number and the date by which the tree must be cut down. It's all highly regulated."

"Just like everything else," put in Bob as he came into the room with cups of coffee.

"If the logs are branded, do you ever have rustlers?" asked Michael.

"As a matter of fact, we do. We call them 'log pirates' or just plain 'poachers,' but it's the same thing. Like anything else where there's something of value, you get in some bad apples who don't like to play by the rules and think they can get something for nothing."

"Have you had any personal experiences with these log pirates?" asked Bob.

"Only once, but I know of others who have. The type of pirates we have now fall into two categories: the firewood types and the full-log types. My experience was with one of the first types. He took down a tree on one of my woodlots, cut it up for firewood, and hauled it away. He didn't stick around to split the wood on site because that would have taken some time, and I might have come by and caught him. However, he did do a good job of trying to cover his tracks by spreading the sawdust out over a wide area and putting old moss on the stump to disguise the recent cut. I never did catch up with him."

"Although it may seem like petty theft to steal firewood, I'll bet the cost to you was more than petty," said Bob.

"Sure. A good timber log can be worth thousands of dollars."

"Do you have any other stories?" asked Michael.

"The one case I know of, again having to do with firewood, is almost comical. It seems two log-truck drivers with full loads left Quadra to go to the mill in Nanaimo. They stopped in Campbell River for dinner at a restaurant on the way out of town. As they were eating, a couple of guys in pickups pulled into the lot behind the trucks, got out their chainsaws and proceeded to cut the ends off all the logs

Chapter Nine

on both trucks, just letting the chunks drop into the beds of their pickups. Then they drove off. Those guys didn't get too far since the truckers came out shortly after the crooks had left and noticed all the sawdust around the back of their rigs and the fresh cuts on the logs. They called the RCMP right away, and the cops found the guys stopped along the road with a sign out saying, "Firewood For Sale." The RCMP took one look and saw the brands on the chunks of wood and hauled them off to the station. The brands, of course, matched the ones on the other ends of all the logs on the trucks, and it was pretty straightforward from there."

"Those two obviously weren't the sharpest knives in the drawer," said Bob.

"Absolutely, but there was another aspect of this that folks other than loggers don't understand. Today when we cut an area, it is almost always under contract to a particular mill. The mill tells us the type of wood they want and the length they want it. We can vary a few inches on the length but not by a couple of feet, which is what these guys were lopping off. Therefore, the logs left on the trucks were now undersize and worth far less than the logs that had been harvested, and the loggers received a lot less money for them than they had expected."

"This is truly fascinating," said Bob. "How about we continue this discussion over an early dinner at the Heriot Bay Inn?"

"You're on," said Mark. "My wife's out of town, so I'd love it!"

Chapter Ten

Mark drove them all down to the inn, and they settled into the pleasant dining room and looked over the menu.

"I hear they have a new chef who's pretty good," offered Mark, "but I always seem to gravitate to the pub menu. Both the fish and chips and burgers are excellent."

"Don't tempt Michael," said Bob. "He may order both."

"C'mon, Dad, I'm not that bad," protested his son.

After their orders were placed, Michael pressed Mark for more stories of the log pirates.

"You said there were two types, but you only told us about the firewood thieves. What about the other type?"

"Well, as your dad noted, the firewood, by itself, is rather petty theft, but the guys who get serious and steal the big timber logs are a different breed of cat. More like burglars and armed robbers."

"We know a little about those types," said Michael.

"Back in the old days, the real pirates would raid some of the rafts the hand loggers were putting together on some of the outer islands. They would cut off from each end what we call a "cookie," a narrow slice of the log that contains the brand, and then simply tow the rest of the log away to a mill. They would put on their own brand, sell the logs, and be gone. If they actually went to the trouble of poaching a tree on someone else's property, they'd simply put their own brand on it."

"Does that still happen today?"

"Not anywhere near as much since the logs have to be a rather specific length to be really worth significant bucks to a mill; plus the thieves still have to have a brand on any logs they sell to a mill, and that can be traced."

"How do they get around that?" asked Bob.

"They get a license to salvage logs and receive a brand code that goes along with that license. We have storms up here all the time, especially in the winter, and logs are breaking loose from rafts all the time. With a salvage license, these guys can pick logs they find floating and deliver them to a mill. They're careful to take only a thin cookie off any logs they steal, but they can turn in other people's logs under salvage without having to change the brand. The way it works now is that if they have a valid salvage license and show up at a mill with a raft of logs, they get paid full value of any with only their brand on them, but they still get half the money for logs with other brands. The half they don't get goes back on a pro rata basis to all the licensees in the area where the log is picked up."

"Boy, it sounds like that's a lot of stuff to go through. There must be some sizable bucks involved to make it worthwhile," observed Bob.

"We're talking some serious dollars, especially when you consider that the thieves get paid for the product and don't have to do any logging themselves. If they're careful and don't get too greedy, they can wait till after a big storm and then show up at a mill with a large raft that contains real salvaged logs mixed in with ones they've stolen," Mark went on. "It would be impossible for a mill owner to sort out stolen logs from ones legally salvaged. After all, the mills aren't the police."

"I can see where this works by stealing logs that are in the water, but do any thefts occur on land on the larger islands?" asked Michael.

"That would get a lot more difficult since the thieves would have to have large logging trucks to move the logs, and crooks don't usually like to operate out in plain sight."

"But if they have to wait for a storm to cover their thefts, don't they have to store the logs somewhere?"

"That's correct, but there are so many little coves and bays around here the RCMP and coast guard don't have the resources to patrol for such things. However, there is one way they could probably move stolen timber that can't even be checked by brand. Once a log has been turned into lumber, the brand is gone. Lumber can be moved around easily and sold to any local building-supply outlet. The only problem with this is that the thieves would need a sawmill. Now, even a small mill can turn out a lot of lumber, so that's not an impossibility, but it would have to be somewhere off the beaten path with ready access to where they are storing the stolen logs."

"Wow, you sure have to have a devious mind to get into the stealing business," said Michael.

"That's why I just do my little thing with my own licenses. It may be hard work, but it has far fewer hassles, and I DO like to sleep nights. However, I did see a recent report from here in British Columbia that the government estimates it loses about twenty million dollars a year in royalties from stolen logs."

They finished their dinners. Bob and Mark just looked at the dessert menu, but Michael said that all this talk of log pirates had made him hungry again, so he opted for a decadent chocolate creation that would have given Jenny Craig fits.

Bob said dinner was his treat, so Mark offered to drive them back to the house and said he would get on the cleanup next week.

Chapter Eleven

Will had been waiting at his computer most of the afternoon on Sunday hoping to hear from his cousin about the extent of the damage on Quadra Island, but it was not until after his dinner that an email showed up in his inbox.

Hey Will,

We really dodged a bullet at the place. It wasn't anywhere near as bad as we'd thought. Lots of brush and broken limbs and shrubs that need to be cleaned up, but Mom's already making plans for what to replant when we get up there. I took a bunch of pictures with my iPhone and have attached a few. As you can see, almost everything is on the part of the property closest to the road, so our great view wasn't impacted at all, and both the house and caboose escaped unharmed.

Will opened the photos and surveyed the scene. Remembering the beautifully wooded area, he could see that there was, indeed, a mess to get rid of, but he was as relieved as his cousin that the damage was relatively minimal.

Michael's email continued:

The cleanup starts tomorrow morning. We have a local logger taking care of it for basically no charge in exchange for the lumber he can get out of the three big trees that came down. Dad and I had dinner with him last night, and he had some GREAT stories about, get this, log pirates! Too much to type it all out, but I'll give you a call this week and tell you the stories.

This last part really intrigued Will, so he shot back an email with a request that the call come sooner, rather than later, in the week. He printed out the pictures his cousin had sent and ran out to share them with his parents, who were in the living room.

"They really were lucky none of those trees hit a building. Look at the size of them. They would have made a mess of the house and probably completely destroyed the caboose if they had hit them," said Doug.

"I guess I know what I'm going to be doing during our visit this summer—helping Angie replant," said Judy.

"Michael says they have a logger starting to put the place back in order tomorrow morning, so it should be all ready for you, Mom, when we get there," said Will.

He then told them about the stories from the logger about the log pirates and that Michael was going to give him a call with the details this week.

"I've never heard of such a thing as a log pirate," said Judy, "Have you, Doug?"

"No, but I'll bet the stories will be fascinating. I hope this doesn't put you and Michael into 'crime stopper mode' even before we get there."

"Oh, Dad, Michael just said they were great stories. He didn't say anything about a crime wave or that we should dust off our RCMP badges."

"Well, I'm sure the stories will be wonderful, and I can't wait to hear them," said Judy.

Chapter Twelve

It was Wednesday evening when the call came in from Michael. Will got his parents together at the kitchen table and put his phone on speaker so they could all hear the stories directly from Michael. The whole family listened to the tales of the log pirates in amazement. No one could imagine such things actually happened, but they realized it was a different part of the world than they were used to, and in spite of the fact there were criminal elements even in an area of such natural beauty, it was still nowhere near the level that they experienced every day in a big city.

When Michael had finished relating the stories from Mark, Doug said, "I certainly don't want to make light of thievery, but some of these crooks are just plain stupid."

"That's exactly what my dad said," responded Michael. "Remember what the man at the hardware store told us about some of the crooks on Quadra who actually called a cab to take them home after stealing a bunch of stuff?"

"I do remember that," said Doug, "But those weren't the types you boys ran across last summer."

"I can't wait for you all to meet Mark. I'll bet he has a few more tales from the woods we would find just as amusing. By the way, my dad has an idea you might want to consider for your trip. He's right here, so I'll turn it over to him."

"Hello, everyone," said Bob. "Hearing the stories of the log pirates triggered something in my memory. There was an article in the *Seattle Times* back in February about the same sort of thing happening here in our national forests, so I went into their online archives and dug out the story. Michael and Angie haven't even seen it yet. I'll email it to you.

"On another subject, however, Angie and I were thinking that it might be fun to have you make a stop in Victoria on your way up to Quadra, after you spend a few days in Seattle. I understand you're planning on staying at the Rainier Club there. You can fly with Kenmore right into the inner harbor of Victoria. The three of us would drive down from the island, meet you there, and at least spend a night before driving back north. The new SUV can seat all of us, even with luggage, since you would still have to pack light for the floatplane. How does that sound?"

"Oh, that sounds grand!" said Judy. "I've heard wonderful things about the old-world charm of Victoria and would love to see it."

"Angie and I love it, too," said Bob. "But Michael has never been there with us, so it would be a new experience for him. We might even have to make it a couple of days. There are some interesting things to see and do there. Since you seem to have developed an interest in the First Nations people, Will, the Royal BC Museum has a marvelous area devoted to them. Butchart Gardens are a must for Angie and you, Judy, especially since Angie has already decided to recruit you for her replanting projects on Quadra. Doug and I might even be able to work in a game of golf. I have a super place for us to stay in Victoria—the Victoria Regent. It's an all-suite hotel right on the water and within walking distance of everything downtown. If you like the idea, I can book us a couple of suites."

"It sounds wonderful, Bob," said Doug. "Let me get our calendars in order so I can give you a firm date, and we'll make it happen."

Both boys were excited about this add-on to their summer adventures and were ready to start doing research on Victoria immediately.

"Hold onto your hats," said Doug. "You both have finals coming up in about a month, so don't get too distracted. First things first." Bob echoed the sentiment, and the cousins slowly drifted back to

Chapter Twelve

reality after being reassured they would have plenty of time to do their research. The phone call ended with two very excited families looking forward to their summer.

Chapter Thirteen

As the school year rushed to a conclusion, both Will and Michael found themselves spread rather thinly. Their baseball and crew after-school commitments and the study load left very little time for further research on Victoria, especially for Will. He did continue his research into the First Nations, partly because he wanted a good grade in social studies but also because, with the cute girl in his class interested in the subject, he got to spend some time with her.

In addition to the collection of Curtis photographs at the Rainier Club, Will also connected with the Burke Museum on the University of Washington campus and prevailed upon his father to work a visit in during their stay in Seattle.

Michael did not have the distraction of a semi-romantic interest at school and thus had some time to look into a bit of Victoria history and sights. He discovered a place he really wanted to go to while the families were in the city: Craigdarroch Castle. His research showed that a timber and coal baron, Robert Dunsmuir, had built the thirty-nine-room mansion in the 1890s. The castle contains over twenty thousand square feet of living area and had originally sat on twenty-seven acres of gardens. That parcel was broken up for development, but the manor is intact and even had restoration work done by a local foundation which now holds title to it.

Chapter Thirteen

Michael discovered the estimated cost of the mansion in the 1890s was around half a million dollars, a phenomenal sum in those days, especially for an out-of-the-way place like Victoria, British Columbia. Digging a bit deeper into Robert Dunsmuir, Michael found that the Dunsmuir fortune was in the range of three hundred million dollars at the time of his death, which would have put him high up on the Forbes list, should there have been one then.

The two cousins continued to email each other as time permitted, sharing the research on their respective topics, but this correspondence came to an abrupt halt when finals week rolled around. By the end of the week of exams, both boys were completely drained, and each slept for nearly two days after school had ended.

As soon as their energy returned, however, they were in full Quadra mode and set about their packing and planning in earnest.

Chapter Fourteen

Michael's family was anxious to get up to Quadra to inspect the clearing and cleanup that Mark had done. He had sent them some photos, along with a statement for his work and the rental of the crane, and they were extremely pleased to see there was no bill and there would be a check waiting for them for three hundred dollars, due to the amount of lumber he was able to salvage from the fallen trees.

Angie was delighted and had already started figuring out what new plants she was going to purchase with it. She phoned ahead to the local garden store in Q-Cove and asked them to put the items aside for her.

Bob had learned his lesson from last year about trying to put too much into their SUV, so the packing of the vehicle went smoothly, and Michael even had room to stretch out his legs.

They were all ready to go less than a week after Michael got out of school and hit the road early for the eight-hour journey. Since the trip required two ferry rides, they did not have to sit in the car the entire time, which made the drive even pleasant. They had a beautiful day and spent almost all the two-hour ferry ride from Tsawwassen to Nanaimo on the upper deck of the boat just enjoying the warm sunshine and fresh air.

Chapter Fourteen

Another two hours from their arrival in Nanaimo, they pulled onto the ferry dock in Campbell River for the twelve-minute ride to Quadra and had already moved on to "island time." Since it was only about three in the afternoon, they stopped at the garden store to examine the plants Angie had ordered. She was very happy with them and said she would be by in a few days to pick them up.

As they came up the road toward their driveway, they noticed it did seem more open but definitely not ruined. As they proceeded down the drive to the house, Angie noticed a large level patch that was still in the sun.

"Look, Bob," she said, "there's a perfect place for a vegetable garden. It would be so nice to have our own fresh veggies right here."

"I think we may have missed the planting season," replied Bob, "but, why don't you check with the folks at the garden store when you go back over to pick up your plants? They may have some things in pots that are ready for planting."

"I'll do just that. Have you two any favorites?"

"Just about anything fresh would be fine with me," said Michael. "As a matter of fact, I could stand something to eat right now."

"When can't you stand something to eat?" asked his father. "As soon as we get the car unpacked, I'll bet your mother could find something to allow you to last till dinner."

"That should speed up the unpacking," said Angie, "and I do have a few nibbles in the cooler."

In less than half an hour, everything from the SUV was in the house and stowed, and Michael was on the deck lying in the sun with a big bowl of salsa and a bag of tortilla chips.

Bob found the check Mark had left taped to the front door and gave him a call to thank him for the good job he had done with the cleanup. Mark said he would come by in the next few days to see if there was anything else they might want to have done in the way of clearing or thinning of trees, and Bob told him they would be delighted to see him.

"I hope he brings along some more stories," said Michael, coming in from the deck with the empty bowl and bag.

"I'm sure he has many. Just don't make yourself a pest," said his father. "Say, how about giving me a hand with getting the deck furniture from the garage and setting it up?"

"No problem," responded Michael. "I'm so glad to be here that nothing seems like a chore. When we finish, I think I'll email Will."

"They're supposed to be in Seattle in about a week and then in Victoria three days later. Make sure everything is still on track, in case I have to change our hotel reservations."

"OK. I'm really looking forward to Victoria. Will and I want to check out that castle and the museum."

Chapter Fifteen

Will had decided to take a stroll over to school to see if his final grades had been posted, more out of old-fashioned curiosity than dread. He was generally satisfied with his grades and knew that his parents would be as well, but he was truly excited about the solid A in social studies he received. He also noted that the cute girl with whom he had studied also got an A, so he phoned her right away.

"It looks like those study sessions on the First Nations we did really paid off. We both aced the class!" Will announced.

"That's great!" she replied. "I never realized the subject could be so interesting. Thanks so much for giving me the insight you have."

"It was fun," Will responded. "I'm actually going back up north again this summer and hope to learn more. We stop over in Seattle for a couple of days and will be staying at the Rainier Club, which has that collection of Edward Curtis photographs. Then, we'll be going to Victoria, and my uncle says the Royal Museum there has a great First Nations exhibit. My cousin and I are going to check it out."

"If you don't mind, could you send me some photos and any information you pick up?"

"I'll be happy to. We will be staying in Victoria for a few days before heading up to Quadra. When we get there, they don't have great cell-phone coverage where my cousin's house is, but they do have satellite internet, so I can email you."

"You've talked so much about this place. I'd love to see some pictures of it too."

"No problem. It's really beautiful."

"How long are you going to be gone this summer?" she asked.

"Probably for most of it, but we'll keep in touch. OK?"

"Absolutely! I want to keep track of my study mate."

Will signed off with a warm feeling and leisurely walked home to tell his folks about his grades.

Needless to say, his parents were pleased, not only with his grades but also with his stated desire to continue his study of the Native Americans over the summer.

After dinner, Will went to his room to send an email to his cousin and found one from Michael in his inbox.

Hey Will,

We just got up to Quadra today and are getting things set up. Dad wants to make sure you all are still set for Victoria, so let me know. The place still looks great. Mom's planning a vegetable garden where the trees came down.

I'll get the boat in shape for us to take cruising when you get here. Don't forget your boaters card. I doubt our dads will pick up the tab for a $250 fine if we get caught without them.

Mark, the logger who did the clearing, is coming over this week. I'll get some more log pirate stories out of him. What did you think of that newspaper article my dad sent?

See you in Victoria in about a week.
Michael

Chapter Fifteen

Will wasted no time in responding,

Hi yourself,

I got an A in social studies because of all the First Nations info I picked from your connection. Thanks much!

We are definitely on for Victoria. I'm sure Dad will get in touch to finalize dates and times to meet.

I'm going to do a little research on the Rainier Club before we get to Seattle. Burke Museum at the UW, too. Have you been to either? The article was amazing. Hard to believe the forest service estimate from ten years ago that poachers stole between $100 million and a cool billion bucks of timber a year!

See you soon,
Will

Michael shot him a quick reply saying he had not been to the Rainier Club but had been to the Burke several times, and he was sure Will would enjoy it.

Chapter Sixteen

Michael spent the rest of the week working on various projects with his parents getting everything in order for when the two families came back from Victoria.

His mother picked up the plants at the garden shop in Q-Cove, and Michael helped her put them in place where she and Aunt Judy would be planting them. His mother also found a few potted vegetable starts of tomatoes, zucchini, chives, and a few other herbs, and these were laid out where the garden was to go.

Michael and his dad turned over the soil in a small area, and the garden was planted. It lasted all of two days. No one had mentioned to them that they needed a deer fence if they planned to get anything out of their little plot. The mother deer and her fawns, however, had a nice meal on the tender young plants and chewed them right down to the ground.

Getting the boat ready to go was straightforward. The motor was de-winterized and started right up. Dad took Michael on a shakedown cruise around Hyacinthe and Open Bays and was pleased with the way his son handled the boat.

Michael scrubbed down the kayaks and made sure everything was ready for him and Will to use when they returned.

The huckleberries were not quite ready, but Michael knew they would be in a week or so, when he would have help in harvesting. Will

Chapter Sixteen

had already confirmed via email that he was ready for some pies and would be glad to help pick.

Mark came over and spent part of one afternoon going around the property with Michael and his dad pointing out some trees that should be taken down before the fall and winter storms came. He told them these trees would not be good for lumber and they should get someone just to cut them down and buck them up for firewood.

"You have a strong young man here who can get a good workout splitting up and stacking firewood," Mark told Bob.

"I'm going to have some help with that, too, I hope," said Michael. "I suppose I could get lucky and have some pirates come along and steal it before I have to split it. What do you think the chances are for that?"

"I seriously doubt that," said Mark. "You're too close to the road, too easy to be seen. Besides, the trees I've indicated to your dad wouldn't be of interest to them."

"Well, do you have any other pirate stories?" inquired Michael.

"I told you the ones I had personal knowledge of, but I'm sure there are more if you ask around. If you're interested in some tales of local hand logging, there's a good book that has many true stories about that, as well as fishing, going back to the late twenties. I think they have copies of it in the bookstore over in Q-Cove. The title is *Heart of the Rainforest*. It's a story about Billy Proctor who's something of a legend in these parts. I think you'd find it an interesting and fast read."

"Gee, thanks. I'll see if it's there the next time we go over. I bet Will would like it, too."

Mark gave Bob the names and numbers of a couple of men who could take down the trees. Before he left, he told Michael, if he and his cousin would like to take a look at a woodlot, they should give him a call, and he would take them along when he went to inspect one of his.

Michael thanked him and said they would probably take him up on his offer in a week or two, and Mark said that would be fine.

The rest of the week seemed to fly by, and before Michael knew it, they were packing the car, lightly, for the drive down to Victoria.

Chapter Seventeen

Will's family had an uneventful flight from Chicago to Seattle and settled into their two fifth-floor rooms at the Rainier Club. Will was delighted to find they were only about four blocks from where they had stayed last summer, so he was in familiar territory.

No sooner had he unpacked his bags than he was walking the halls of the club admiring the vast collection of Curtis photographs. He also found in the lobby a rack where copies of them were available for purchase.

Judy discovered the Health Club, also on the fifth floor, and was quick to book a massage for the next afternoon. She also wandered the halls and various rooms enjoying the rest of the club's large art collection. The gallery had a current show of a local artist, which Judy found most inspiring. The land and waterscapes reminded her of the area around Quadra Island, and she discovered that was the exact locale the artist had used for inspiration.

Doug spent time with the concierge arranging for a car and driver for the following morning to take them to the Burke Museum, making sure they would be back in time for Judy's massage. He also booked dinner in the club for that evening and was told their rooms also included a continental breakfast. He informed the concierge there was a teenaged boy in their party, and he hoped the club would

Chapter Seventeen

not lose too much money on the breakfast. The concierge laughed and told him that there would be plenty and not to worry about it.

They all went for a little stroll down to Pioneer Square and back to stretch their legs after the plane ride and returned for an early dinner and bedtime, considering the two-hour time change and the fact they wanted to get an early start in the morning.

The next day dawned bright and clear, and their car showed up exactly on time. Their driver took them on a leisurely drive on surface streets, rather than the freeway, to the university. They went around Westlake, crossing the Lake Washington Ship Canal via the Fremont Bridge, and the driver showed them the popular sculpture of *Waiting for the Interurban*. People had dressed the figures in party hats and put up a sign with "Happy Birthday – Marcia" on it. Then the driver turned up the hill and went under the north end of the Aurora Bridge and showed them *The Troll*, another local favorite outdoor sculpture featuring the giant troll's hand wrapped around a full-size Volkswagen Beetle.

They all loved these whimsical works of art, and Will snapped lots of photos on his iPhone to send to the cute girl back in Chicago. They arrived at the Burke Museum just as it was opening. Outside, they viewed several intricately carved totem poles, and inside, they looked over the de Menil collection of a thousand images of Northwest Coast totem poles.

Will found the "Pacific Voices" exhibit of particular interest, especially the Northwest Coast ethnographic collection and the Alaska Arctic collection. He also picked up information on the collections of artifacts from the Plains and Great Lakes regions, which he thought would also be of interest to his study-mate in Chicago.

They spent several hours in the museum and left in time to have lunch before getting back to the club for Judy's massage. Their driver told them he would take them to Ivar's Salmon House, an iconic local restaurant, on the ship canal. They had a wonderful meal and then returned to the club.

After Judy's massage, the family walked around the downtown area and then ventured to the International District and found a good Chinese restaurant for dinner. Even Will was full after this meal, and they cabbed it back to the club.

"The driver showed them The Troll, another local favorite."

Chapter Seventeen

The next day, they decided to do one of those obligatory tourist things and went on a Ride the Ducks tour, which included some time on the water. They thought it was pretty hokey but joined in the laughing and singing and had a good time anyway.

It was another early night, since they had an 8:00 A.M. Kenmore flight to Victoria. This time, they left from Lake Union, right at the north end of downtown, and the flight was only an hour.

Coming into Victoria by floatplane was a memorable experience. Landing in the bustling Inner Harbour required impressive piloting skills. There must have been a dozen little water taxis putt-putting around the harbor, plus a lot of other boat traffic, and there were two other regularly scheduled floatplane airlines serving the harbor. They motored to the dock at the Adventure Center, picked up their bags, cleared Customs, and asked directions to the Victoria Regent. They were only three blocks away.

Chapter Eighteen

Will and his family walked along Wharf Street to the Victoria Regent Hotel and down through the lovely garden to the lobby. As they checked in, the general manager came out from his office and greeted them, "You must by the group from Chicago."

"We are, indeed," said Doug. "Is it that obvious?"

"Not really. Your brother, Bob, called and told us to expect you about this time. We have two suites all ready for you on the sixth floor, and your brother insisted we put you into the Executive Suite. His family will be right next door."

"That's marvelous," said Judy. "This is a perfect location. I hope we have a view of the harbor."

"Absolutely," replied the manager. "It was also mentioned that you two gentlemen might like to get in a round of golf while you're here."

"That would be ideal," replied Doug.

"Just let me know which day, and I can arrange that for you. I assume you will need to rent clubs, since you arrived by floatplane."

"I think we probably both will since Bob didn't mention he was bringing his with him. I hope not because it will make it a bit cramped on the drive up to Quadra with all six of us and luggage."

"Your brother and his family should be here in about two hours, so why don't you get settled in? The bellman will take your luggage to the room."

Chapter Eighteen

They found their room at the very end of the hall on the sixth floor, and the bellman showed them the door to the room next door where Bob, Angie, and Michael would be staying.

Their suite had two bedrooms, a full kitchen, a fireplace in the living room, and a deck overlooking the harbor, and the master bath even had a Jacuzzi tub, which Judy said she would definitely try out. They unpacked and took a few minutes just to sit on the deck and enjoy the view.

"Those little water taxis look like fun," said Will. "They seem to go all over the harbor. We should take a ride."

"Why don't we do that?" said Doug. "We have a couple of hours before the others arrive, and it'll give us a bit of a feel for the city."

"Look," said Will, pointing, "they even stop right here at the hotel."

The family returned to the lobby and were told how to get down to the float where the water taxis docked. When they boarded, Doug asked that they be given a full harbor tour, and the pilot gladly obliged. They started off down toward the Adventure Center where they had landed, and their guide pointed out the stately Empress Hotel and the Parliament buildings. Will asked about the Royal BC Museum and was told it was right across the street from Parliament.

They then cruised around the harbor and all the way out to the docks where the big cruise ships came in. Coming back, they headed straight for their hotel and then turned under a bridge and proceeded up a gorge into what appeared to be a more industrial area. It was not as scenic but did give them an idea that this was not just a tourist town. By the time they bumped up against the float at the Regent, almost two hours had passed. As they got out of the water taxi, they heard a call and looked up to see the other family waving to them from the deck next to their suite.

After joining them and a round of hugs and handshakes, to absolutely no one's surprise, both boys said, "What's for lunch?"

"We have dozens of choices within an easy walk, including some right across the street," said Bob. "What do you feel like?"

They all settled on some basic sandwich, soup, and salad fare, and Bob said there was a good place for all those right on Government Street, just two blocks away. "And then we can stop by Roger's

Chocolates for dessert after lunch," offered Bob, and they all headed out the door.

Chapter Nineteen

After filling up two starving teenagers, the families discussed plans for the rest of the day. The boys wanted to go to the museum, Angie wanted to show Judy some of the shops on Fort Street and Trounce Alley, and Bob and Doug said they would make reservations for dinner and set up their golf game.

They set up a five o'clock meeting time back at the hotel, and Bob gave his Family Pass to the museum to Michael. The boys headed off in one direction, while the adults went the other. On the way to the museum, Michael and Will walked through the lobby of the Empress.

"This hotel used to be owned by the Canadian Pacific Railway, which built fancy hotels like this all across Canada along their routes," explained Michael. "Now it's owned by Fairmont, which also owns the Olympic, where you stayed in Seattle last year."

"I can see some folks might like the charm of a place like this," said Will, "but I really like where we're staying."

"Me, too," replied Michael. "This is a bit stodgy for my tastes."

The boys stopped to look over the fare at the High Tea being served. They thought it looked OK until they happened to notice the price.

"Wow," said Will, "isn't that a bit high for cucumber sandwiches and a bowl of strawberries?"

"You bet! If this is what they get for tea, I don't think our dads are going to be bringing us here for dinner."

"That's fine with me."

"Likewise. Let's go to the museum."

The boys crossed the street, entered the front doors, showed their pass, and went up the escalator to the exhibit areas, picking up a guide map on the way.

"Let's start with the First Nations exhibit," suggested Will, and Michael readily agreed.

They found the entire exhibit fascinating, including the cutaway earthen lodging and the long house. The mask exhibit was huge, and they were truly impressed by the intricacy of the carving and the many different animals and spirits represented. They discovered an area of argillite carvings from the Haida tribes in the area around and north of Quadra. These also displayed the great skill of the carvers. In their exploration, they came upon a small TV screen showing a portion of *In the Land of the Headhunters* and spent several minutes watching it.

From this exhibit, they moved into the Old Town exhibit and the dioramas of some of the early industries of the area. The mine and fish-packing plant were of interest, but the sawmill and logging displays had a special appeal due to their recent exposure to stories of log pirates. From these, the boys moved on to the natural history exhibit. Although Will had been to the huge Field Museum in Chicago, he told Michael that these dioramas were even more realistic than the ones back home. They went into the Open Ocean exhibit, which was almost like an amusement park ride, but both thought it was very cool. By the time they finished their tour, it was almost five, so they made their way back to the Regent.

When they got back to their rooms, they found their parents there and assembled in the large suite, sitting on the deck.

"Hi there," said Doug. "Did you find the museum interesting?"

"It was seriously cool," said the boys, simultaneously.

"That's great," said Bob. "I thought you would like it."

"Say," said Doug, "we were thinking that we might rearrange the room assignments so that you two could have the suite next door, and the adults would all bunk together here. That way, since Bob and I are

Chapter Nineteen

getting up early for golf tomorrow, we won't disturb you, and you can watch movies until all hours of the night without disturbing us."

"That's fine with me," said Will, and Michael enthusiastically agreed.

"We thought you'd like that, so we already moved your things, Will, into one of the bedrooms next door," said Judy. "Now, what would the two of you like for dinner?"

The boys said they had been so wrapped up in the exhibits at the museum that they had not even given it a thought. Although their parents found that hard to believe, they made them another offer.

"If you two would like to be on your own tonight, the four of us felt it would be nice to have a quiet dinner at a wonderful little French restaurant right across the street from the hotel," said Bob. "We'll give you money for dinner, and you can go wherever you'd like."

"Michael, I know you like Chinese food," said Angie, "and Chinatown is just about three blocks away. Don Mee has really authentic food and is a fun place to go. How about that?"

"Fine with me," said Michael. "How about you, Will?"

"No problem here," said Will. "By the way, they sure aren't, or at least weren't, politically correct around here, are they?"

"What do you mean?" said Judy.

"Well, at the museum we saw a mockup of an old fish-packing plant. It was very realistic, including sounds of gulls and waves, but there was this machine they used to scale the fish, and printed right on the side of it was 'The Iron Chink.' That would be pretty offensive today."

"Times certainly change," said Bob, "and sometimes those changes are for the good. I'm glad you boys recognize that."

"They have a very active Chinese community here in Victoria," put in Angie. "An auxiliary of the Lions Club here, called the Lady Lions, has as its president a woman who is on the Victoria City Council. That certainly would not have happened even twenty or thirty years ago."

"Brother Bob," said Doug, "I'm truly impressed. You and Angie are really up on what goes on with your neighbor to the north. More Americans should pay better attention to the world outside their own little circle."

"Well, we figure it's just part of being a good neighbor. If we don't spend at least a little time getting to know our closest occupant of this continent, then how can we expect to deal with others around the world whose cultures are radically different from ours?"

"A very good point; I'll try to remember it."

"Well, this has gotten a bit heavy," said Judy. "Why don't we freshen up and get ready to go to dinner? We can continue our international goodwill conversation over some fine French cuisine."

Chapter Twenty

Michael and Will relaxed in what was now their suite and tided themselves over till dinner with a few snacks from the minibar. They had gone to the front desk and picked up a walking map of downtown Victoria and had scoped out Chinatown and found out where Craigdarroch Castle was. Since their dads were going to be off playing golf, they figured they would have to walk to the castle, but it did not look to be that far, as long as they had enough breakfast to sustain them on the trip.

It was still bright and sunny when they emerged from the hotel and started off in the direction of Chinatown, even though it was already past eight. The lady at the desk had told them they could not miss Don Mee, right on Fisgard Street, which ran through the middle of Chinatown. They found the restaurant with ease and climbed the stairs to the dining room. The place was almost full, but they found a place for two and noticed nearly all the patrons were Asian.

"This must be good if all the locals eat here," observed Michael.

"Why don't we try letting our waiter just bring us what he thinks is best? It might be a bit of a surprise but probably worth it," suggested Will.

"That's a great idea!"

Their waiter arrived momentarily and offered them menus. When Will told him to just make their choices and keep bringing food until they said, "Enough," he smiled and said, "I will make sure you are both full and happy when you leave."

An hour and a half later, when their waiter came with one more dish, both boys said, "Enough!" emphatically. They were able to finish the last plate, however. When the bill came, they were both pleasantly surprised; it came to only a little over half what their fathers had given them. They left a generous tip, pocketed the fortune cookies for later, and headed out into the warm evening.

The street was still a beehive of activity and brightly lit, so they decided to explore. Across the street from the restaurant, they noticed a sign that read "Fan Tan Alley." It marked a crack between two buildings that was so narrow they had to walk single file. The alley was lined on both sides with shops displaying an array of exotic and mostly unidentifiable items. It was so interesting that when they popped out on the next street, they turned around and went back to Fisgard just to experience it again.

At the far end of Fisgard, they could see a huge gate, decorated with dragons and Chinese characters, so they walked up to inspect it further. As they passed through the arch, they found themselves on Government Street, so they walked back down it towards where they had had lunch. Passing the street that would take them directly back to the hotel, they came upon a broad walking area noted as Bastion Square. They turned into it and strolled back toward the water, noticing the Maritime Museum on their way to Wharf Street.

They were just passing a small Italian coffee shop when they saw a sign in the window—gelato. The boys looked at each other, shrugged, and went inside. The cones were gone before they walked the final block to their hotel.

Chapter Twenty-One

The next morning dawned bright and clear. Bob and Doug had already left for their golfing outing by the time Michael and Will rolled out of the sack. Their mothers had rapped at their door to see if they would join them for the complimentary continental breakfast at the hotel. Never needing much encouragement to partake of food, the boys told them they would be down within five minutes and proceeded to get dressed and to the restaurant.

Although only a continental breakfast, similar to the one that Will had at the Rainier Club, he assured Michael it would give them enough sustenance to make the trek to the castle. While their mothers watched in awe, both of them started with a bowl of cereal and juice, then moved on to croissants with peanut butter and jam, two hard-boiled eggs, topped off by a large cinnamon bun washed down with a cup of hot chocolate.

"My goodness," said Angie, "you two must have consumed in one meal what one person in a Third World country would in a year."

"If we were staying any more than two days, the hotel might have had to rethink its 'free breakfast' policy," put in Judy.

"Well, we're going to be doing a lot of walking today. After the castle, we may try to work in a tour of the Parliament building," said Michael.

"We ladies are going to hop on a double-decker bus and take a ride out to Butchart Gardens for the day," said Angie.

"This evening we thought we would all go out for Italian. We found what looks to be a very nice restaurant close to where we were for dinner last night," said Judy. "It's right off Waddington Alley."

"Boy, this is a strange town," said Will. "I've never been anyplace where they name their alleys. We found another one ourselves last night."

"We discovered Fan Tan Alley," added Michael. "Have you been there, Mom?"

"Oh yes. It's marvelous," replied his mother. "If we have time after we get back from the gardens, I'll have to show Judy."

Angie and Judy excused themselves and said they wanted to make sure they made the bus, but the boys hung around surveying the harbor over one more cup of cocoa.

The boys returned to their room to grab a light jacket and their city walking map and then struck out for the castle. On the way up Fort Street, they looked in all the windows of the shops and went into one with the unlikely name of BC Shaver and Hobbies, which was crammed to the rafters with models of all kinds. Kits of ships, planes, boats, cars, and trucks were stacked high on the shelves, and many completed models were hung from the ceiling. Farther up the street, they found a coin-and-stamp shop, which also dealt in military paraphernalia, so they had to stop in there, too.

It was well past ten when they finally reached Craigdarroch. They paid their admission fee and joined with a tour, which was just starting. They learned that the castle had undergone many transformations over the years, serving as a school and a hospital at various times, until the foundation took it over and began the restoration. When the formal tour was finished, they were encouraged to explore on their own and told not to miss the climb up into the turret.

The view from the top was spectacular. Michael pointed out a large snow-covered mountain in the distance and told Will it was Mount Baker in Washington.

"But that looks like it's north of us, if my sense of direction hasn't completely left me," said Will.

Chapter Twenty-One

"The view from the top was spectacular."

"It is," replied Michael. "The international border dips down to divide the Strait of Juan de Fuca, which is that body of water you see to the south. The southern tip of Vancouver Island, where we are now, is quite a bit south of the northern border of Washington. It's a bit weird, but not as strange as a little community called Point Roberts, which sits at the end of a peninsula and is part of the US, although the rest of the peninsula is Canadian."

"It's a good thing we're friends with Canada," said Will, "or the folks who live there could be mighty uncomfortable."

After spending most of the morning at the castle, the boys headed back down to the main part of town to take a look at Parliament. They had noticed the night before that the entire building was outlined in lights, which gave it a rather whimsical appearance— almost like Disneyland.

The Legislature was not in session, so they were allowed to take a peek into the chambers and wander around the halls. Over one doorway, they noticed an intricate stained-glass window that looked to be the flag of the province of British Columbia. However, it was not quite right, so they asked a guard about the difference.

"Well, you see, lads," the guard explained, "the window was commissioned for this legislative building when it was built. The artist made it in what was the logical fashion. Since British Columbia is the westernmost province in British North America, he put the setting sun on top, and the Union Jack below. The British government pointed out that there could be nothing on any provincial or national flag of a Commonwealth nation that was placed above the Union Jack, so our flag had to be changed. However, they did let us keep this window."

"That's amazing," said Michael. "Do you have any other unusual stories about the building?"

"I don't know if you noticed in the legislative chamber, but the seats for the opposing parties are arranged across a center aisle facing each other. In the States, the opposing parties are on opposite sides of a center aisle but face the podium. In our building the spacing of the center aisle has a particular feature in that its width is two and a half sword lengths. It gives you an idea of how fierce some of our political debates can become."

Chapter Twenty-One

"That is too weird," said Will. "I can't wait to lay that one on my dad."

With all sorts of interesting news to share with their folks, the boys decided it was time for lunch and then a relaxing stretch-out on the deck.

Chapter Twenty-Two

That night's dinner was a jovial celebration of stories from the three different adventures of the day, including golf tales, gardening tips, and the history lesson from the boys. As predicted, both fathers enjoyed the revelation about the spacing of the seats in the legislature, which prompted several cynical jokes.

Although the time in Victoria was enjoyed by all, they wanted to get up to Quadra and so decided to leave right after breakfast. Bob and Angie told the others the ride up would start out with some spectacular views from Malahat Drive, which would take them up about a thousand feet above a fjord.

They set a time to meet in the restaurant the next morning and adjourned for an early night to get packed for the trip north.

They had another beautiful day for their drive, so Bob said he would stop at the top of the Malahat so the boys could take some pictures. They proceeded on through Duncan and Ladysmith and passed by Nanaimo, and Bob told them it would be about another two hours before they were on Quadra.

This last part of the trip was on the Inland Island Highway, which gave them only glimpses of the water. Bob said the Oceanside Route was much more scenic but it would add at least another hour to the drive, so he had opted for the fastest way.

Chapter Twenty-Two

Unfortunately, they pulled onto the ferry dock in Campbell River just as the ferry for Quadra was pulling out of the slip. Since they had an hour to kill before the next boat, the boys said they had noticed a sign on the adjacent dock advertising "the best fish and chips in town" and suggested checking out its claim would be a good way to spend the hour.

They wandered down the ramp to the fish-and-chips place and were just finishing their meal when the *Powell River Queen* came around the end of the breakwater and lined up on the loading dock. They hustled back to the car knowing they were now only half an hour away from their very special destination.

Both boys spent the twelve-minute ferry ride out on deck sucking in the fresh salt air and trying to decide what they would do first when they arrived. Michael thought a boat ride was in order and conveyed that to his father. Bob said that would be fine, but the boys did not have unlimited gas credit for the summer.

The two fathers agreed that they would pick up the tab for gas for any of the approved overnight camping trips but the boys were on their own for any cruising around they wanted to do.

"The kayaks are in good working order," said Bob, "assuming you two have the energy to propel them. Given the amount of food you put away, I can't imagine you will be lacking in that regard."

"We know there're lots of places we can go in the kayaks," replied Michael, "and we'll use them for most of them, but if we want to go up to the end of the island or over to Cortes, that's too much of a paddle."

"No problem there," said his dad. "I just want us to be on the same page on this."

With the ground rules established, both fathers agreed that the boys could take off right after unpacking and settling in.

"I would like to go along on this first one," said Doug. "I want to make sure Will feels comfortable with handling the boat. After all, he didn't get the hands-on experience you did, Michael."

The boys were fine with this, especially when Doug said he would not horn in on their entire cruise, so they could drop him off at the float after a brief demonstration.

When the car pulled up in front of the house, Will and Michael piled out and headed for the caboose with their bags. Doug said he would join them in about fifteen minutes on the float.

Chapter Twenty-Three

Since Bob had previously checked Michael out on the operation of the Whaler, he did not go along with Doug and the boys. Doug returned in about half an hour to report that all seemed well. The boys had their iPhones, so they could call home if they were in an area with coverage and ran into any little problems. Doug said both boys knew what to do in a major emergency and could use the radio to call the coast guard and any other boats in the area.

Doug said he had checked out the tool kit on board with Will, and his son told him it looked as if it was complete enough for him to do any repairs should they have motor problems. Doug reported their sons were going to cruise up the channel where they first had spotted the yacht used by the burglars they had encountered last summer. They had promised they would be back at the float no later than seven.

"I know that little channel," said Bob. "Angie and I have gone through it a number of times. It's one of the prettiest spots around. The four of us will have to take a spin up there ourselves and also go into Crescent Channel behind Bold Island. That's a lovely place where the fellow who has the shellfish lease out in front of us here grows all his mussels and a lot of his oysters."

"That would be fun," said Judy. "I've never seen a real oyster farm."

"Well, all you can see are the floats the oyster strands are attached to, but it is an impressive operation."

Angie and Judy set about dinner preparations while the men took it easy on the deck and rehashed yesterday's golf game.

"I don't completely get this golf thing," said Judy, "but Doug seems to be able to play the same round over about a dozen times if he has someone to compare notes with."

"Oh, Bob's the same way. I guess it makes them feel they really get their money's worth if they play it more than once, even if the other times are only in their minds."

"I do notice a similarity to fish stories, however. The drives seem to get longer and the putts shorter with each telling."

"Funny you should mention," said Angie, laughing.

Michael and Will appeared right on schedule, already washed up and ready for dinner. Afterwards, they helped their mothers clean up the dishes and said they thought they would grab a movie to watch in the caboose before turning in. They said they had noticed a fairly good patch or two of huckleberries down by the boathouse and would pick enough for a pie for tomorrow's dessert. Their mothers agreed it was a fair exchange and promised the boys would not be disappointed. With that, the rather long day came to a close.

Chapter Twenty-Four

The next week seemed to fly by. There were hikes, kayak trips, boat rides, berry picking, and of course, fantastic meals and spirited games of Monopoly. Near the end of the week, the boys called Mark to ask if they could accompany him on a survey of one of his woodlots. He said he was going to be heading up the island on Sunday afternoon and would be happy to stop by and pick the boys up on his way.

Mark pulled into the drive about one thirty and was introduced by Bob to Angie and the Chicago group. He accepted an invitation to have a cup of coffee with the two families, and they pulled up chairs on the deck.

"I have to tell you," said Doug, "we were absolutely fascinated by your stories of log pirates. We had never heard of anything like that in Chicago. Of course, we have far more than our share of other criminal elements, but his was a new wrinkle."

"Well, I hadn't thought much about them lately, either, since I lost that tree to a thief for firewood. As a matter of fact, I'll show the boys exactly where it was today. Until Michael asked about branding and rustlers, it probably hadn't come to mind in a year or so. By the way, I do have one of my branding mauls out in the truck; I'll show it to you before we take off for the woods."

"Can we see how you use it?" asked Will.

"Sure, there's an old stump or two we can whack, but I'm not bringing down any new trees today. This is just a survey trip."

"You told us about the guys who steal whole logs. Have you had any cases of that lately?" asked Michael.

"It's funny you mention that," said Mark. "Because you brought the subject up, I wondered if that freak storm that blew down your trees had maybe broken loose some log rafts and scattered some sticks. It turns out quite a few of the small loggers in the surrounding islands reported losing a significant number of logs. I thought that sounded a little strange since the wind storm was so localized and centered primarily right here on Quadra. So I called a few friends at various mills from Campbell River down to Nanaimo to see if any large rafts of salvaged logs had shown up for sale. None of them had seen any salvaged logs since last winter, which made me think the storm might just have been used as cover for stealing some logs."

"But if that's the case," put in Michael, "you'd think they would have turned them into cash."

"That would normally be true," Mark went on, "but if these guys happen to have gotten greedy without having any salvaged logs to sell for six months or so, they might be cutting them up for lumber to maximize their take."

"However, as you noted when you told us this in the first place," said Bob, "that would mean they'd have to have a sawmill hidden away somewhere and they'd have to have someplace to store the logs out of sight."

"Absolutely," said Mark, "but I haven't heard about any large sales of lumber, and I certainly don't want to get into the investigation business; that's up to the RCMP. I did call their station here just to see if any thefts of logs had been reported to them and was told 'nothing out of the ordinary,' so I guess that's about where we are."

"It certainly makes for good conversation, though," said Doug.

The coffee having been finished, Mark said he and the boys should get going so he could have them back in time for dinner, and they all walked out to his truck. Digging into the back, he brought out what looked like a small sledge hammer. The head was a cast aluminum piece with some letters and numbers on it.

Chapter Twenty-Four

"These symbols indicate both the woodlot, or lease number, and the date by which the timber must be cut. You can't sell any logs with this brand on them after the date shown. As you can see, this one is still in effect, but I do have an old one somewhere here in the truck, and you boys can have it, if you like."

"That would be super!" said Will, and Michael enthusiastically agreed.

"OK. Hop in the truck, and we're on our way. We'll be back in a few hours."

Chapter Twenty-Five

On the way to Mark's woodlot, they passed the trailheads for Morte Lake and Chinese Mountains where they had hiked last summer. They drove on until the road forked and then veered off to the left.

"We took that other road last summer to go swimming in Village Bay Lakes," said Michael.

"If you continue on it, you will come to a steep road that goes down to a little beach near Surge Narrows," said Mark. "It's pretty rugged up that way, but quite beautiful."

"Where isn't it beautiful around here?" said Will.

"Good point," said Mark.

They continued north up what was now a dirt road toward Granite Bay at the far end of Quadra Island. As they entered a densely wooded area, Mark said, "It's just up ahead. See that sign on the left? It has the lot number and some information about the timber management in this area."

They pulled over and got off the road as far as they could. "I wouldn't park like this during the week. This is an active logging road, and the big trucks really come barreling along here. However, we're in good shape on a Sunday afternoon."

Mark grabbed the branding maul, and they all piled out of the truck.

Chapter Twenty-Five

"The brands were deep and clear."

"There's a bit of a trail right here," said Mark. "Don't go wandering off. These woods are very thick, and it's easy to get disoriented and lost. Even I've thrashed around in here a time or two when I didn't pay attention to where I was going."

They had not gone more than about fifty feet from the road when Mark pointed to a stump right off the trail.

"It looks pretty old, doesn't it? Well, look closer. See how the moss isn't really attached to the stump. It was just put there to disguise the cut when it was fresh. If you look just here," Mark said, pointing again, "you can see a depression in the ground. That's where the tree fell. The sawdust from the bucking cuts has long since gone back into the earth, but I was able to spot it when I first found the tree was gone."

"How did you ever notice the tree was missing?" asked Michael.

"I know my trees," said Mark. "They're like children, although I don't go so far as to actually name them."

"That's amazing," said Will.

"Well, while we're right here, why don't you boys take a whack with the branding maul at the top of the stump?"

They both gave it a try and admired their work. The brands were deep and clear.

"That's a pretty good brand," observed Michael, "but it doesn't appear to go too deeply into the wood. I would think thieves could just cut a sliver off the end and put their own brand in place." "They could, and probably do if they are out to sell the log for the most money. Remember I told you we have to cut to size? However, wood has a property that allows old brands to be seen, even if they don't appear on the surface. The maul compresses the wood fibers quite deeply into the log. X-rays can bring out the original brand, even if several inches have been cut off. I also understand that heat can do the same thing, but portable X-ray equipment is pretty handy nowadays. Most of the mills have such gear, which they use if they suspect stolen logs are being presented to them, but they don't do a 100-percent scan, and they really have to have a serious suspicion to do one at all. If logs arrive with a valid salvage license brand on them, they are hardly ever given an X-ray test; at least that's what I've been told by my friends at the mills."

Chapter Twenty-Five

They went a little farther into the woods, and Mark checked out a few trees and spotted some underbrush he said he would clear out on another trip. The boys asked how large this woodlot was.

"Ten hectares. That's about twenty-five acres to you," Mark informed them.

"How do you go about logging this lot?" asked Michael.

"When I get ready to harvest," said Mark, "I bring in some equipment, put in a narrow road just wide enough to let me haul out the logs, and cut a ways in on each side of the road. We don't clear-cut these areas any more."

He told them timber in a full logging truck would be worth between $4,500 and $6,000 for fir and cedar but only about $3,000 for hemlock. He also explained that this one was a very small woodlot and that now some of the woodlots run up to eight hundred hectares, or nearly two thousand acres.

Mark asked if they had any more questions, and the boys said they had absorbed about as much as they could for a one afternoon's logging lesson. They piled back into the truck and headed back to the house ... and dinner.

Chapter Twenty-Six

That night at dinner, the boys regaled their parents with the logging information they had picked up from Mark. Michael also got out the book Mark had told him about, *Heart of the Rainforest,* and told them a few of the stories of Billy Proctor. Will and his parents said they would like to read it after Michael finished. Doug and Judy said perhaps Will could take it back to Chicago for them to read since they might not have time on this trip, needing to be getting back in about a week.

"In that case," said Bob, "we had better see if these two young men can get in their first overnighter on the boat before you leave so you can have a feeling of security about their safety."

"That would be wonderful," said Judy. "I'm sure everything will be just fine, but I would feel better if I saw you safely home after your first adventure."

After dessert, they adjourned to the living room to look over some maps and charts and decide on the destination for the boys' cruise and camping trip. Bob noted there was a lovely sheltered moorage on Cortes Island called Von Donop Inlet that would be a great place to both cruise and explore.

"There is a nice beach at the end of the inlet. You could camp there and then take the forest trail over to the other side of Cortes. It comes out in part of Squirrel Cove."

Chapter Twenty-Six

"Do you think we could tow the two-person kayak along with us so we could explore the inlet without burning up all our gas allowance?" asked Michael.

"As long as you take it easy on the speed with the Whaler, I think that would be fine," said Bob. "The weather's supposed to continue warm and sunny for the next four or five days, so you may not even want to pack a tent along, maybe just a tarp."

"If you leave after breakfast, I can pack a cooler with what you'll need for a couple of lunches and one dinner and breakfast," said Angie.

"I'll also make sure there'll be some assorted munchies, along with a fresh batch of cookies," put in Judy.

With the destination now set, the boys were all ready to leave the next morning, but their parents put them off for one more day.

"I want to make sure the extra gas cans are full and we have a chance to go over your checklist of equipment," said Doug. "Besides, your mom needs a little time to bake those cookies."

"I see your point, Dad," said Will. "We certainly don't want to be caught short on cookies."

Two mornings later, with one of Judy's special pancake breakfasts under their belts, their gear all stowed on the Whaler, and the kayak securely tied on behind, the boys set out into Hyacinthe Bay on their way to Von Donop Inlet. They cruised out around the Bretons and up the Sutil Channel between Read and Cortes Islands.

Finding the entrance to the inlet, they cruised slowly inside. They passed a stream coming down over some rocks and made note to come back and explore it. At the end of the inlet, they found the beach Bob had described, and it did indeed look to be a perfect campsite. There was not a single boat in the entire inlet, so they beached the Whaler and set up camp, having the entire beach to themselves. The next order of business, of course, was lunch.

Over the next twenty-four hours, they paddled every cove in the inlet, hiked the trail to Squirrel Cove, explored the stream up to its source, a beautiful lake that was, however, too cold for a swim. They slept under the stars and marveled at the sight of the Milky Way unimpaired by city lights.

By the time the next afternoon rolled around, they were down to their last half dozen cookies and decided it was time to head home, not without a feeling of accomplishment.

Chapter Twenty-Seven

With the boys' safe return, Doug and Judy were at least psychologically prepared to return to their home, although they had found the allure of Quadra to be every bit as strong as it was for Bob and Angie. It was an emotional farewell at April Point a week later as Doug and Judy boarded the Kenmore Air flight back to Seattle.

The boys settled back into their routine of kayaking, berry picking, swimming, and working in the occasional boat ride. The blackberries along the road began to ripen, and the huckleberry pies were now alternated with blackberry, with no decrease in enthusiasm on the part of two hungry teenagers.

About ten days after Doug and Judy returned to Chicago, the boys began planning their next overnight adventure. This time, they said they would like to go to the Octopus Group. Bob and Angie were not quite as sure of this trip since the boys would have to negotiate Surge Narrows. Bob went online to get the tide tables for the passage for the next few days and went over in detail the procedures for getting through the narrows at slack tide.

"OK. I think you have the basic principles down," said Bob, "but I want to go with you for a practice run. We can hit a slack tomorrow at ten thirty. Can you be ready to go?"

"Absolutely!" said Michael, and Will echoed with enthusiasm.

They headed out the next morning allowing plenty of time to traverse the Hoskyn Channel up to Beazley Pass, the entrance to Surge Narrows. Bob wanted to get there while the tide was still running so he could show the boys what it looked like when slack occurred. They were able to hold their position just outside Beazley Pass and watch as the standing wave in the middle of the channel got smaller and smaller and finally disappeared altogether. At that point, Bob piloted the boat through the narrows, making sure both boys could see the whirlpools and eddies still present even at slack.

When they had passed through, Bob made a wide turn and brought the boat around for a return through the narrows. This time he turned the controls over to Michael.

"Keep a firm grip on the wheel," said Bob to his son. "You can see how turbulent the water still is at slack. You can imagine what it must be like when it's running at about fourteen knots."

"Wow!" exclaimed Michael. "I can really feel the pull, even in our little boat. I imagine it would be even stronger for a boat with a lot more draft."

"Of course, larger boats do have more power and larger steering rudders, but you are absolutely right."

When they had passed safely through the narrows and into the calm water around the little group of islands called the Settler's Group, Bob said, "That was very well done. I think you can handle it on your own. How would you like to take a slight detour on the way home and go through Whiterock Passage and around the north end of Read Island?"

"Is the gas on you for this one?" asked Michael.

"Sure," said his dad, laughing.

The trip through Whiterock was just as beautiful as both boys remembered. Although the water was extremely calm, the channel was also quite shallow, and they had to line up navigation markers both fore and aft, making a turn in the middle.

They motored out into Calm Channel and then into the north end of Sutil Channel, passing by the entrance to Von Donop Inlet on their way back.

As soon as they bumped up against the home float, both boys said they were having some hunger pangs, so they hurried up to the

Chapter Twenty-Seven

house to see if Angie had something to ease the pain. She had a large tray of sandwiches, bags of chips, and cans of soda all ready as the trio came through the door.

"They did great!" announced Bob. "I guess they can finalize their plans for the overnight to the Octopus Group."

Chapter Twenty-Eight

Michael and Will spent the next day and a half putting together everything they wanted to take. This time, they decided to take a small camp stove and the tent so they could have a hot dinner and keep off the morning mist. Because there was so much to see and explore around the Octopus Group, they prevailed upon Bob and Angie to make it a two-day outing.

Since they would have to go through Surge Narrows, they opted not to take the kayak but brought along two spare cans of gas so they could motor around the area.

It took three trips down to the float to get everything assembled for loading into the Whaler, but they were able to get it all stowed and secured. They planned to go ashore on one of the small islands in the group and set up their camp so they would not be hauling all their stuff around on their explorations.

They had their iPhones, and Bob remembered there was coverage where they would be, so Michael promised he would call his folks after they got their camp set up. With that, they cast off the float and headed north.

Having allowed plenty of time before slack tide, the boys took a slight detour through Crescent Channel behind Bold Island and surveyed the oyster and mussel farm. The man who had the shellfish lease on the area in front of their house was out on one of his large

Chapter Twenty-Eight

"Unloading their gear..."

floats, so Michael pulled in to say hello. The man showed them around the float and then sent them on their way with an invitation to return any time.

The passage through Surge went smoothly, and they cruised up the Okisollo Channel at a leisurely pace enjoying the scenery in the fresh air and sunshine. When they reached their destination, they found a number of large pleasure craft in the main portion of the marine park and a few in some of the larger coves.

After surveying the scene, they backtracked slightly and found a small island with a gravel beach where they could bring the Whaler up. Unloading their gear, they hauled it to a little clearing among some evergreens, set up the tent, and broke out lunch from one of the coolers Angie had packed for them.

"This is definitely the life!" said Will sitting in the soft moss and leaning up against a big fir.

"No doubt about it," echoed Michael. "I see we have almost three bars right here, so I'll give the folks a call and let them know we've made it OK."

"Don't forget to thank your mom for the food."

"Will do. Those sandwiches were great. That must have been a new bread recipe she used."

The call having been made and the parents reassured, the boys set about charting their explorations for the next couple of days. Michael remembered there was a new park established on Quadra that ran from the end of the bay next to the marine park all the way over to Granite Bay on the other side of the island, so they decided to take the boat to the end of the bay and see if there was a trail to hike.

They found the trail and started along it. After about an hour of fairly difficult hiking, they decided to head back to the beach where they had left the boat.

"It may be a park," observed Michael, "but they sure could do some work on that trail."

"It was almost like an obstacle course with all those fallen trees," said Will.

"Well, it just helps to work up an appetite for dinner. Mom didn't think we could survive on my cooking, so our dinners have been prepared and only need heating."

Chapter Twenty-Eight

"I'm sure your mom made something great, so I'm not worried."

"When we get back to our camp, why don't we cruise around all the tiny islands right there? The channels between them are shallow, but we'll just take it slow and raise the motor up a bit."

"Sounds like fun. I'm game."

The rest of the afternoon and early evening was spent exploring their immediate surroundings. They went ashore on another island and walked to a house Michael remembered from a previous trip with his family. It was abandoned and missing all its doors and windows, but it contained the most amazing collection of mobiles and other works of questionable artistic merit.

"Boaters come here and put up these creations," explained Michael. "If you look around, you can find two or three from the same boat that have been left over the years. They're all pretty goofy, but it's become a tradition."

"I'd say it looks as if these folks have way too much time on their hands."

Chapter Twenty-Nine

Back at their camp, Will set up the stove while Michael unpacked dinner from the cooler.

"Hey! Wow! Lasagna and garlic bread," exclaimed Michael, "and not a salad in sight."

"I'll just put some foil over the whole stove, and we'll have a little oven," said Will. "It should be ready in no time."

As it turned out, it was also gone in no time, along with half a tray of brownies and a quart of milk.

They checked to make sure the boat was secured on the beach and tied to a large tree and then settled back and watched the moon rise over the Coast Range.

"Tomorrow, let's cruise back down the channel and check out the shoreline of Quadra," suggested Michael. "Usually coming down this channel, we're heading to Surge, so the focus is straight ahead, but now we can take some time just to look around. It's not built up along here because there aren't any roads, except for the one that Mark told us about going down to Surge, and that's on the other side of the narrows."

"That's fine with me," said Will. "We can just take it easy."

With tomorrow's schedule firmly in mind, the boys crawled into their sleeping bags and gazed out the tent flap as the moon rose and their eyelids fell.

Chapter Twenty-Nine

The sun rose with a vengeance the next morning before six, and try as they might, the two young men could not stay asleep. After a breakfast of bacon and eggs, which started out as fried but ended up as scrambled, and some of Angie's special bread toasted over the flame of the camp stove, the boys were ready to start out on the day's journey.

They hugged the shore as they moved down the channel. Trees came right down to the water's edge and hung over the granite boulders making a sort of tunnel in places. There was not a lot to see, but they did cruise around the shallows in Yeatman Bay and then back out along the shoreline toward Surge Narrows. Michael pointed out a group of small islands on the Quadra side of the narrows.

"We're just about at slack, and the currents shouldn't be too bad, so I'd like to go around those little islands. I know from the charts that no boats go in there because there are too many rocks and no real channel, but they look interesting to just putt around in."

"OK, but I'll keep an eye out for rocks, and you keep your eye on the depth sounder. We've been doing great so far; let's not bend a prop."

"I'm with you on that," said Michael.

Surprisingly, there was almost no current around the little islands; most of the water was funneled through the narrows, where it was much deeper. They did a slow cruise around the tiny lumps of rock and then turned around at Peck Island to go back toward Octopus. As they headed back, they saw a small cove on the shore of Quadra they had not noticed when they had first come into the group of islands.

"Hey," shouted Will, who was on lookout on the bow, "check out that cove. It's filled with logs!"

Carefully watching the depth sounder, Michael maneuvered them close to the mouth of the cove. As they approached, they could see that the mouth had been sealed off by a large log boom, anchored to the shore on each side with massive chains.

"Get us up against that boom," said Will. "Let's take a look at those logs."

Michael dropped a fender over the side and bumped the Whaler up against one of the huge logs sealing off the mouth of the cove.

"That's quite a harvest of logs," observed Will.

"Check out the ends of them; they all appear to be branded."

Timber Treachery

"...check out that cove. It's filled with logs!"

Chapter Twenty-Nine

"Yeah, but all the brands are different."

"I'll bet these are the ones Mark told us about that disappeared from the rafts of the small loggers after our freak storm."

"You're absolutely right. These have to be stolen. What else would explain all the different brands?"

"I'll hold us steady on this log," said Michael. "Take some pictures with your iPhone of the ends of as many logs as you can get a clear shot. I'm sure Mark could figure out where they all came from."

"If these are all stolen logs, the crooks couldn't take this big a raft into a mill without arousing suspicion. Do you suppose they plan to turn them into lumber and sell them off that way?" asked Will.

"That must be it," replied Michael, "but that means their mill must be somewhere nearby."

"Let's go around the point and see if we can find a place to tie up and do a little exploring on shore."

After taking a few photos, they pushed off from the log and motored around the point at one side of the cove. The bank along the shore was steep, but they found a small crack in the boulders that had a tiny beach, and they carefully guided the boat in by hand. Tying it up to a large tree branch, they scaled the bank up to the woods and made their way back in the direction of the cove. The woods were thick, which made for slow going, but they finally came out on a bank overlooking the cove filled with logs.

"Wow, there have to be hundreds of them," Will noted.

"That is a lot of money," observed Michael. "Let's get a few shots of the whole scene from here."

Moving around the bank above the cove, the boys took a number of photos and were just about to return to their boat when they heard a gasoline engine start up somewhere in the woods above the cove. They took cover behind some trees and none too soon. Out through an opening in the trees on the shore of the cove that was nearly invisible came two rather rough-looking men dragging a steel cable. One of them grabbed a pike pole, which was stuck in a fallen tree near the water. He maneuvered one of the logs onto the shore, and the two of them put the cable on the end of the log. One of the men hiked back up the trail into the woods. In a few minutes the sound of the engine increased, and the log moved off the beach and up through the woods.

"Let's get out of here before we're spotted," whispered Michael.

"You're not going to get an argument out of me," responded Will.

When they got back to their boat, they were both sweating and out of breath. They untied the Whaler and worked their way back out of the little crack in the rock. Neither said anything until they were well underway back to their camp.

Chapter Thirty

"How come we're in this beautiful place with so many nice people around but we seem to run into the bad guys all the time?" asked Will as they pulled up on the beach by their camp.

"I don't know. Maybe it's our magnetic and irresistible personalities," answered his cousin.

"Yeah, that must be it, but where do we go from here?"

"Well, my immediate feeling is that we should beat it home and tell my dad, and probably Mark, what we just found and let them and the RCMP handle it."

"I couldn't agree more. Those guys we saw certainly weren't Mafia types, but they looked pretty rough anyway, and I sure don't want to take them on, especially on our own."

"No problem with that, but the tides aren't right for us to make it home until tomorrow morning, so I guess we'll have to stay here for the night. My phone is still showing about three bars, so we can at least let my folks know what we saw, and they can get something started."

"That's right," said Will. "Besides, we still have a bunch of food to take care of. We wouldn't want your mom to think we didn't like her cooking."

"Spoken like a true scholar! You can get us some lunch, and I'll call home."

Michael placed the call, but it went immediately to voicemail. Not wanting to leave his parents a message that might cause them to worry, he simply said they were having a great time and had an interesting story for them, should they get a chance to give him a call back.

After a hearty meal, the boys decided to stick close to their camp for the rest of the day. They did take the boat into the main part of the marine park, giving it a complete examination. They went ashore on the small island in the middle of the park and enjoyed checking out the little creatures in the tidal pools on one side. As the sun dipped behind the big trees, they motored back to their camp to go over what they had seen.

"I think we must be right in our assumption that they are cutting those logs into lumber," said Will. "The sawmill must be back in the woods where they were hauling that log."

"The area is certainly remote enough that the noise of the mill wouldn't be noticed by anyone, but it also must have some access for them to be able to get the lumber out," observed Michael.

"Mark said the only road up this far on this side of Quadra ends at the Surge Narrows beach, so they must have access to it somewhere."

"If we hear back from my folks, we can ask them to have Mark or the RCMP check for an access road, but I'd sure like to get those photos of the logs to Mark before we send anyone off on a wild goose chase. He'd have a good idea from the brands that the logs were stolen, but I don't have an email address for him."

"Your folks have email, though. You could send the photos to them," offered Will.

"That's true, but I don't want to alarm them until we have a chance to talk to them."

"OK. Let's just enjoy another dinner here and a good night's sleep, and we can head back when the tide is right, even if we don't get a call back tonight."

"That sounds reasonable to me. This is a comfortable place, and I don't think we have a problem with those guys back there. I can't imagine they saw us."

The stove was set up and the cooler emptied of everything that wouldn't be needed for breakfast in the morning. After a huge meal,

Chapter Thirty

the cousins sat back and again watched the moon rise until they crawled into their sleeping bags and nodded off.

Chapter Thirty-One

The boys awoke to another beautiful morning in the Octopus Group and set about preparing a breakfast of everything that was left in the cooler. They figured they could make it home by lunch and have something fresh when they got there.

They had no sooner rinsed off their dishes in the salt water than Michael's phone rang.

"Good morning," came Bob's cheerful voice. "How are you both doing this lovely day?"

"We're fine, Dad," replied Michael. "I see you got my message."

"Yes. I'm sorry we didn't get back to you sooner, but your mother and I went over to Campbell River to a movie and caught the last ferry back to Quadra. By the time we got home and listened to your message, we felt it was too late to call."

"That's OK, but we do have some interesting news. We found a cove full of logs that we think have to be stolen. We took some pictures of the brands on the logs. I'll send them to you as soon as we hang up. Will you get them to Mark? I'm sure he can tell by the brands where they came from and if they're stolen."

"I'm glad to hear the Quadra Island Crime Fighters Association never sleeps," joked Bob. "I'll be happy to send the photos to Mark. I'll give him a call and let him know to expect them. In the meantime,

Chapter Thirty-One

you boys don't do anything stupid. Just get yourselves back here and don't do any more snooping around."

"We learned our lesson last year," said Michael. "We were going to break camp and load the boat when you called. I think the tide will be just right for Surge by the time we get there. We should be home for lunch. Do you think Mom can whip something up?"

"The Quadra Island Teenage Feeding Association never sleeps either. I'm sure she will have a meal ready for you when you get here."

"Thanks, Dad. We'll see you soon."

It did not take long to pack the tent and sleeping bags, and the coolers were much lighter for the return trip. They filled the gas tank from one of the spare cans and had the Whaler ready to push off in a half-hour. They motored out into the Okisollo Channel and back toward Surge Narrows, this time keeping well out from shore.

When they reached the narrows, the water was about as slack as it ever gets, and the passage went smoothly. However, just as they came through Beazley Passage, around from the back side of Peck Island came another boat moving very quickly and on a course directly toward their midship. Will took a quick look through his binoculars and exclaimed, "Hey, those are the guys we saw on the beach of the cove yesterday! It looks as if they want to ram us!"

"I think you're right. That guy in the bow also has a pike pole."

"I don't think we'd better stop," said Will. "Do you think we can outrun them?"

"They have a really good angle on us. I'm not sure. But, I have an idea. Hit the deck and hang onto the mountings for the seats and get set for a wild ride."

Michael kept to his course but increased his speed gradually. The other boat was now closing fast and showed no sign of slowing or changing course. Suddenly Michael yelled, "Hang on!" and turned sharply so the Whaler was now aimed directly at the bow of the other boat. A head-on collision was moments away when the man in the bow of the other boat noticed what was about to happen. Not wanting to take the full force of the impact, he shouted to the driver and waved his arms frantically. At the very last instant, the driver of the other boat swerved sharply to avoid a collision, which would probably have sunk both craft.

The man in the bow was thrown off his feet and over the side of the boat. Michael only slightly altered course to miss him and kept going down Hoskyn Channel at full throttle. By the time the other driver had turned his boat, returned to his partner, and hauled him back aboard, Michael and Will were almost out of sight.

Chapter Thirty-One

"The man on the bow was thrown off his feet and over the side..."

Chapter Thirty-Two

"Wow! That was some bit of boat driving, cuz!" exclaimed Will when they were safely away from immediate peril. "Where did you pick that up? I didn't see a chapter on it in the BoatSafeCanada literature."

"What? That was just a friendly little game of chicken," said Michael with a smile.

"Easy for you to say. You were in the stern."

"I did tell you to get low and hang on, didn't I?"

"Sure, but at that speed, I don't think I would have been in great shape."

"I was actually counting on the guy in the bow of the other boat to come to that conclusion. He had to realize he would have been a sure goner if we had hit."

"Well, so much for OUR conclusion that we weren't seen at the cove yesterday. I wonder why they waited till now to make their move."

"Maybe they only caught sight of us as we were leaving and didn't have time to stop us then. After we'd gotten back to camp, there were other boats around, and they probably didn't want any witnesses to whatever rough stuff they had in mind," said Michael.

"You're probably right. If they had rammed us back there in Beazley Passage, it would just have been a boating accident, not foul play."

Chapter Thirty-Two

"We should be home in about fifteen minutes at this speed," said Michael. "I wonder if my dad got the photos to Mark."

They kept the throttle down until they came up to the Bretons and turned into the channel to go past Open Bay and into Hyacinthe Bay and then slowed to let the motor cool down before they got to the float. They tied up the Whaler and carried the coolers, now filled with not-too-clean dishes, and the camp stove up to the house, leaving their gear on the boat to stow later.

As they approached the house, they saw Mark's truck in the drive and quickened their pace. Dumping their load by the door to the kitchen, the boys went out onto the deck, where Bob, Angie, and Mark were seated at the table.

"Those are some VERY interesting pictures," said Mark as the boys pulled up chairs. "I definitely recognize at least three of the brands as belonging to some small logging operations I know from the islands. I was able to get in touch with two of them, and they confirmed some of their logs have been recently stolen, not just broken loose from their rafts."

"I think we are able to provide corroborating evidence," said Will, and he started to describe their close call. The boys alternated telling parts of the story, while Bob and Angie sat in stunned silence.

"Dad," said Michael finally, "I want you to know we didn't go back to do any more snooping around. Those guys just came after us."

"I believe you, son," said Bob, "but I think it's now time to bring in the authorities."

"I agree," said Mark. "I think I recognize those men from your description. I don't know them personally, but they have a reputation of getting into fights and just being undesirable types. Best to let the Mounties handle it from here. Their mill must be somewhere back in the woods off the Surge Narrows road, but I sure don't want to go looking for it. They have to have access to a main road to get the finished lumber out, and I'm sure the RCMP won't have any trouble finding it."

"Bob, why don't you call that nice officer we met last year and have him come out and hear Mark's information and the boys' story?" said Angie. "I'll put out the lunch I have all prepared."

"I'll do that right now," said Bob, getting up from the table. "Mark, you just take it easy right where you are. The boys can get out plates and silverware."

Chapter Thirty-Three

The five of them had just finished lunch when the police cruiser pulled into the drive. The RCMP officer joined them on the deck for some cookies and coffee. Bob had given him only a brief rundown on the telephone, so he asked Mark and the boys to fill in the details.

"In looking at the brands on the logs in the boys' photos, I was able to identify several and contacted the loggers that I know," Mark began. "The two I was able to reach were absolutely positive that the logs were stolen since they hadn't experienced any rough weather where they were."

"However, they don't actually have any proof of that, do they?" asked the officer.

"No," said Mark, "but I notice on the logs in the pictures there is only one brand on the ones where I can actually make out a brand. If these guys had actually salvaged them, they would have put their own salvage brand on them right away. I think that indicates that they didn't intend to take them to any proper mill and share payment for them with the rightful owners."

"That makes perfect sense," said the officer, "but it's only circumstantial. They can easily claim they were just too busy salvaging and were waiting to apply their brand later."

"So I guess if they're cutting the logs into lumber, thereby eliminating proof of ownership by someone else, that's just circumstantial as well?" asked Mark.

"Unfortunately, that's the case."

"Well, what about trying to ram us in the boat?" put in Michael.

"Do you actually have any proof they were trying to run into you?"

"I wasn't taking time to film it," said Will, "but it was pretty obvious."

"However, here again, it's your word against theirs. There were no witnesses to the incident. They could just as easily claim that you were a couple of crazy kids playing around and trying to run into them."

"If that were the case, why would we call you?" asked Michael.

"To cover your tracks in case they reported you for unsafe behavior on the water."

"Omigosh!" exclaimed Will. "Isn't there anything you can do?"

"The legal system has its procedures. We aren't quite as limited in what we can do as our compatriots in the States, but we still are governed by the rules of evidence. It doesn't do anybody any good if we arrest these guys on charges that can't possibly hold up in a court of law."

"You didn't have any trouble taking decisive action last year," noted Bob.

"That was a very different situation," said the officer. "When people are holding others against their will by gunpoint in front of witnesses, it makes our job a lot easier. By the way, Mark, simply forget you just heard the last part of this conversation."

"OK, I don't have any idea what you all are talking about anyway."

"In any case," continued the officer, "I certainly believe the three of you that you have uncovered something here. I know these small loggers have a tough enough time making a living without having to deal with people like these. What I can do is send out an unmarked car with a plainclothes officer to see if he can locate the access road to their mill. If we can determine for sure that's what's going on, we'll come up with some way to get the evidence we need to make an arrest. Meanwhile, please don't put yourselves in harm's way by doing investigations on your own," he said, looking at the boys.

Chapter Thirty-Three

Michael and Will nodded in agreement, and Mark said he was happy with what the officer had suggested. The officer promised he would let them all know if he discovered the location of the mill and fill them in on what the police were going to do about it. Everyone seemed satisfied with that, and the officer left.

Chapter Thirty-Four

About a week went by before they heard again from the RCMP officer. He reported they had located the access road to the secret mill and had done some very careful reconnaissance without arousing any suspicion on the part of the thieves. He told them the police were formulating a plan and would like to meet with all of them, including Mark, to make sure they had all the facts straight before they put it into operation.

They got together the next day at Bob and Angie's, and the officer laid out what the RCMP had in mind.

"We have obtained a warrant to have someone wearing a transmitter and recording device make contact with the suspects. We want to assure ourselves that the exchange results in satisfactory incriminating statements by the suspects. Mark, we want to run some questions by you to make sure we're using proper logging terms so as not to arouse their suspicions."

"I assume the person will just 'happen upon' the mill and start up a conversation, right?" asked Mark.

"That's correct," responded the officer, handing Mark the list of questions they had come up with to elicit the responses they wanted.

After looking over the list, Mark said, "I don't see anything wrong with the questions themselves, but I could imagine this going south in a hurry if they start to push back on any of them."

Chapter Thirty-Four

"What do you mean?" asked the officer.

"Well, the questions seem structured like an interrogation, and I think you would have a better chance of getting what you want if the questioning takes more of the form of a conversation. If they start to ask questions of their own, your man is going to have to really know what he's talking about not to give himself away."

"None of my officers is a logger. How do we give them a crash course?"

"I'm not sure you can, not knowing what the suspects might bring up. I think you need a real logger to pull this off."

"Are you volunteering?" asked the officer.

"It's definitely not my first choice," responded Mark, "but quite a few of those stolen logs belong to some of my friends, and I'd like to help out."

"That is gratifying," said the officer. "We could use some expert assistance."

"I assume I wouldn't just be strolling in there on my own, would I?" asked Mark.

"Absolutely not! We'll have armed officers in the woods on both sides of you at all times."

"It sounds as if I was already set up for this," noted Mark.

"We were hoping," responded the officer. "If we can get enough incriminating evidence on tape to justify making an arrest on theft charges, we were also hoping that we could arrange a confrontation with the boys to bring more serious charges. However, we aren't keen on having them be the first contact, and we're sure their parents wouldn't be either."

"You've got that right," said Bob and Angie simultaneously.

"However, a confrontation with the boys might get the men to let something slip about the attempted ramming of their boat that could serve as a confession."

"About the only way we could agree to something like that is if you assure us that these guys would be cuffed and restrained before they ever get a glimpse of the boys," said Bob.

"You have my word," said the officer.

Bob turned to the boys. "Would you two be willing to do that?"

"No problem," said Michael, and Will nodded emphatically.

"We'll finalize the details in the next day or so and let you all rehearse your roles before we go in."

Chapter Thirty-Five

Two days later, Mark, the RCMP officer, and the boys gathered to make the trip to the Surge Narrows road. Mark was dressed as a fisherman, complete with pole, creel, and a hat covered with tied flies.

"We already have men in the woods on both sides of the road into the mill," said the officer. "Mark, here's your transmitter-recorder. All my officers and I are tuned to your frequency, and we also have recording devices, just as a backup. This will fit easily into your hat, and you don't have to do anything to activate it; it's already transmitting."

"OK, let's do this thing before I get too nervous and back out."

They all piled into the officer's car and headed up the road. On the way, the officer reminded the boys that they were to stay with him until he had received word that an arrest had been made and the suspects were securely restrained.

"If something goes wrong, or we don't get enough evidence to make the arrest, these men will never see you two. If all goes according to plan, the three of us will simply walk down the road and face them. Neither of you should say anything; let them do the talking. If we're lucky, they'll make a stupid statement confirming the attack on you, and we'll have additional charges to bring."

The boys nodded assent, and the rest of the drive was in silence. When they reached the Surge Narrows road, the officer slowed the car, and they proceeded quietly to the side road that had been cut into the woods for access to the mill. The thieves had put a gate on the road and a sign saying "Private Property – Keep Out." The officer pulled a bolt cutter from the trunk and snapped the padlock off the gate.

"These guys have a lot of nerve; this is Crown Land, not private property. I'll have to check to see if we can add yet another charge."

The officer pulled his car onto the road, effectively blocking it, and Mark started strolling along down toward the mill, pole over his shoulder. The boys stayed with the officer and quietly waited for the transmission from Mark when he came upon the thieves. They did not have to wait long.

"Hey, you," came a harsh voice over their earpieces, "where do you think you're going?"

"Fishing," said Mark as casually as he could.

"Didn't you see the sign? There's no trespassing here."

"I didn't see any sign. I just came upon this road going through the woods down to the water."

"Well, just turn around and beat it!" came another voice.

"Oh come on, guys, I don't mean any harm. Just let me go down to the beach and get a few of these flies wet."

"Head right back up the road and find another way down to the water," said the first voice.

"Gosh, it looks like you fellows have a nice little sawmill going here. I didn't see any signs that there were any woodlots around here," said Mark, trying to deflect the conversation.

"Just mind your own business," said the second voice, "and get going."

Mark stood his ground and tried to look clueless. "Those are some nice logs you have there. Did you log them around here?"

"Yeah, we did," came the first voice again, this time even harsher. "What's it to you?"

"Oh, nothing. I just see that the two logs you have right by the saw bed have different brands on them; I just thought that was a bit unusual."

"I said that's none of your business," came the second voice, and it was obviously agitated.

Chapter Thirty-Five

Mark kept the conversation going as long as he could, getting the two thieves to say they had a salvage license and had picked up the logs in the water, contradicting their previous response to his question about logging the timber themselves. When Mark happened to mention that he did not see a salvage brand on the logs, things turned nasty. One of the men apparently picked up a weapon of some sort and physically threatened Mark. At this point, the officer with the boys radioed his men to move in, and they could hear quite a bit of loud, angry yelling and sounds of a scuffle.

When all was quiet, one of the officer's men radioed him to say the suspects were cuffed and that he could bring the boys down.

Both Michael and Will were a little nervous, even though they were being escorted by the officer. When they came out into the clearing by the mill, the two suspects spotted them.

"Hey, Harry, it's those snoopy kids who were around here last week," said the second voice.

"Shut up, Sam," said the first voice.

"We should've taken care of them right then," said Sam.

"I told you to shut up," said Harry.

"But, oh no, you said to just wait and make it look like an accident."

"Keep your mouth shut," growled Harry.

"Hey, it was easy for you. You were just driving the boat; I'm the one who got thrown overboard," Sam snarled back.

At this point, the officer with the boys said, "I think we have enough. Let's haul these men down to the station."

While most of the other officers herded Sam and Harry back up the road, two went off into the woods to retrieve the vehicles they had brought. The other officer, Mark, and the boys stayed at the mill site to look around.

"This is a sweet little operation," said Mark. "There are thousands of dollars worth of cut lumber in that shed next to the mill. They've even done a good job of camouflaging both the mill and shed. You'd have a tough time spotting them from the air."

"Let's assume that they really do have a salvage license. There should be a branding maul around here someplace," said the officer.

"Hey, Harry, it's those snoopy kids..."

Chapter Thirty-Five

It did not take very long to find the maul, and Mark said it would be easy to trace. The code on it showed it was valid, but Mark wondered if even the maul might have been stolen.

They went down to the cove, filled with logs, and Mark did an inspection of most of them.

"I think it's pretty obvious that they were going to turn these into lumber rather than trying to sell the logs. None of them have the brand of the maul we found, so the crooks didn't even bother to mark them as they would have to do in order to sell them at a legitimate sawmill."

"It's still circumstantial, but with the threat to you and the confession of the attempt to ram the boys' boat, I think there is a preponderance of evidence that will stand up in court," said the officer.

"There is one nice part of all this," observed Mark. "Since they didn't put another brand on the logs, they can be returned to their rightful owners."

"We'll have to hang onto them until we certify the evidence, but that shouldn't take too long. We'll make sure we verify ownership and contact the people involved and expedite the return of their property."

"All this excitement has really made me hungry," said Michael. "What say we get back to the house for a little lunch?"

With that, the four of them returned to the officer's car and Michael's home.

Chapter Thirty-Six

Needless to say, Bob and Angie were greatly relieved to see their son and Will back safely and insisted that Will call his parents before he filled his mouth with food.

While Will was on the telephone, Angie prepared a special meal for the crime fighters, which included fresh baked rolls and a big pot of clam chowder with some huckleberry tarts for dessert. Bob, Mark, and Michael sat on the deck with the RCMP officer, and he and Mark filled Bob in on the events of the morning. Mark admitted he was very nervous when Sam had picked up the pike pole and pointed it at him and welcomed the timely arrival of the Mounties riding to the rescue. He, along with the officer, also praised Michael and Will for really keeping their cool when confronting the thieves.

When Will returned from the call to his parents, all six of them enjoyed a relaxing lunch, and the conversation lightened up.

"I was actually relieved with the hostile reception," said Mark. "My biggest fear was they would welcome me in and want to join me fishing. That would have blown the whole thing. I don't have the faintest idea how to fish!"

"I'm glad you didn't tell me that before," said the officer. "I would've been nervous, too."

Finally both Mark and the officer said it was time they got on with their respective jobs and excused themselves, thanking Angie

Chapter Thirty-Six

for the delicious meal. Bob helped Angie clean up the dishes while the boys crashed in the deckchairs and took a nap.

The next few days passed in relative serenity. The boys picked some more huckleberries and dug several bags of clams, which they hung off the float. They took a short boat ride around Read Island but avoided Surge Narrows. One afternoon, they packed a lunch and paddled the kayaks down to Rebecca Spit and came home around the Bretons.

When they returned that afternoon, they found the RCMP cruiser in the drive when they came up from the float and the officer with Bob and Angie on the deck.

"Ah, there you are, lads," said the officer. "I just stopped by to let you know what's going on with those two log pirates. The magistrate feels we have adequate evidence to file charges and take this to trial. He set bail high enough that there's no way they can raise it, so they'll stay in jail until their case comes up."

"That's a relief," said Michael. "I'd hate to have them walking around looking for Will and me."

"I doubt that will happen in any case, even after they serve their time. Quadra is like a small town, and folks here don't take kindly to people who steal from their neighbors. Besides, if they come back here, I'll bet there will be more than a few irate small loggers who might like to have a little talk with them. Of course, we couldn't sanction anything like that, but we might never hear about it."

"Well, that's a relief for all of us," said Angie.

"There's another reason I stopped by," said the officer. "Once again, I would like to thank you young men for your civic-mindedness and your courage. I know you have your official badges, and we don't issue oak leaf clusters for them, but I want you to know we feel you richly deserve them."

"I really appreciate that," said Will, "and I know Michael feels the same way."

"You bet!" put in Michael.

When the officer left, Angie said, "You boys have earned another special dinner. What would you like?"

Both boys opted for barbequed hamburgers, French fries, and a big salad, followed by Angie's fabulous brownies with ice cream. Bob made the trip to the market, and one more fantastic meal was shared on the deck.

Chapter Thirty-Seven

The days began to get shorter and cooler, and both boys realized that the summer was coming to an end. With only about ten days left before the start of another school year, they got the house and caboose buttoned up for the winter, packed their bags, loaded the SUV, and bid a fond farewell to Quadra until the next visit.

Both boys spent the entire twelve minutes of the ferry ride to Campbell River on the back deck of the boat looking at Quadra with a real feeling of sorrow. The drive back down to Nanaimo was quiet, as were the ferry ride to Tsawwassen and the journey back to Seattle.

Will spent the night with Michael and his family before catching a flight to O'Hare the next day. He dozed off and on the whole flight reliving in his mind the fabulous adventures of the past several months. He was feeling rather melancholy until another thought popped into his mind. He sure would have some great stories to tell that cute girl in his class when he got back.

About the Author

Bruce Bradburn and his wife, Meg Holgate, an accomplished landscape artist, live on First Hill in downtown Seattle, Washington. They also have a home on Hyacinthe Bay on Quadra Island in British Columbia, which serves as the home base for Bruce's stories.

Bruce has lived in Seattle since 1947 and has owned the home on Quadra since 1997. He has a degree in industrial engineering from Northwestern University in Evanston, Illinois, and owned an electronics firm in Seattle for thirty-five years until his retirement in 2001.

He spent a number of years working in local politics and spent a year in the Washington State Senate in 1980. He has also been involved in a number of hotel ventures and is current chairman of the board of the Victoria Regent Hotel in Victoria, British Columbia. He also runs the Quadra property as a seasonable bed and breakfast.

He is a devout theatre lover and has served on the board of trustees of Intiman Theatre and is currently on the board of the Seattle Repertory Theatre.

Bruce enjoys cooking, especially with any of his three children and nine grandchildren. Food always plays an important role in his stories.

About the Author

He also is somewhat of a car nut and raced vintage automobiles for a dozen years, retiring from that hobby in 2004.

These stories attempt to open young eyes to the natural beauty of the Pacific Northwest and to instill a sense of appreciation and respect for the wild creatures who inhabit the area, as well as the First Nations people, who were the first stewards of the land and seas.

Appendix

These family recipes of the author are favorites of visitors to Quadra Island.

Will and Michael's Favorite Brownies

Ingredients
7 oz. good bittersweet chocolate
7 tablespoons butter at room temperature
1½ cups firm-packed light brown sugar
4 extra-large eggs, slightly beaten
½ teaspoon real vanilla extract
½ teaspoon almond extract
½ cup all-purpose flour
⅔ cup unsweetened cocoa powder
1 cup sliced almonds, plus more to sprinkle over top of batter

Preheat oven to 350°.

Grease an 8 X 10-inch baking dish; cover the bottom with waxed or parchment paper.

Break up the chocolate and place in microwavable bowl. Microwave for 20 seconds, stir, microwave again for 20 seconds. Repeat this until the chocolate is completely melted and smooth. Be careful not to over-microwave. Set aside until needed.

Put the butter and sugar in a mixing bowl and beat with an electric mixer until fluffy. Gradually beat in the eggs and then the vanilla and almond extracts. Then beat in the melted chocolate. When thoroughly combined, sift the flour and cocoa into the mixture and stir to combine. Fold in the nuts and transfer to the prepared pan, spreading evenly. Sprinkle additional sliced almonds over the top of the batter and bake in the preheated oven for about 20 minutes or until almost firm to the touch. NOTE: ovens vary, so adjust cooking time accordingly. Remove pan from oven and cool on rack.

The author wishes to acknowledge ***Brownies*** by Linda Collister (Ryland Peters & Small, Inc., 2006) as providing the inspiration for this recipe. It has had several ingredient and quantity changes to accommodate the particular tastes of the author and his grandchildren.

Chili Egg Puff with Black Bean Sauce

Puffs

Ingredients
6 eggs
1 pint cottage cheese
1 cup Bisquick
2 small cans diced green chilies
1 small onion, diced
1½ pounds grated cheese (Cheddar, jack, aged Gouda, Asiago, etc.)
Optional: *1 or 2 diced jalapeno chilies, red or green*

Grease (or spray) 8 4-ounce ramekins

Mix all ingredients until thoroughly combined and pour into ramekins. Chill for at least 1 hour before cooking. NOTE: the ramekins may be covered with plastic wrap and frozen for future use—thaw before baking. Bake in 350° oven for about 45 minutes. Remove from oven and cool slightly before serving. Top with cherry tomato halves and fresh chives. Serve with fresh salsa and Black Bean Sauce (recipe follows).

Black Bean Sauce

Ingredients
¼ large yellow onion, diced
2-4 garlic cloves, diced
1 tablespoon olive oil
1 14-ounce can stewed tomatoes, partially drained and chopped
1 14-ounce can black beans
1½ teaspoons ground cumin
½ teaspoon cayenne pepper
1 teaspoon chili powder
3 tablespoons chopped fresh cilantro

Brown onion and garlic in oil. Add tomatoes and cook over medium heat until volume is reduced by about half. Add black beans, cumin, cayenne, and chili powder. Cover and cook for 15–20 minutes. Stir in cilantro just before serving.

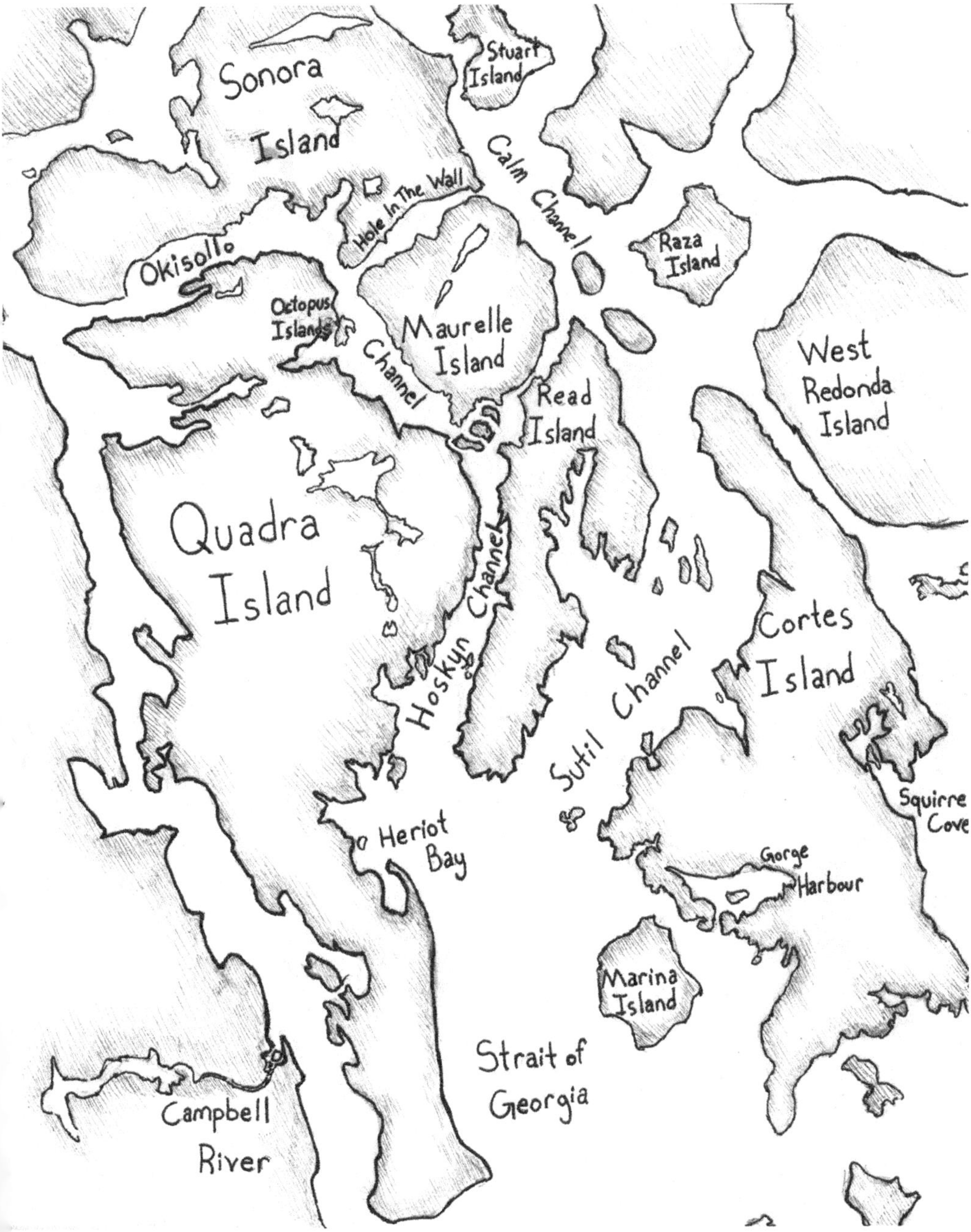
Sonora Island
Stuart Island
Calm Channel
Hole In The Wall
Okisollo
Raza Island
Octopus Islands
Maurelle Island
Channel
West Redonda Island
Read Island
Quadra Island
Hoskyn Channel
Cortes Island
Sutil Channel
Squirre Cove
Heriot Bay
Gorge Harbour
Marina Island
Strait of Georgia
Campbell River